Love Unexpected

Love Unexpected

RITU KAKAR

Srishti
PUBLISHERS & DISTRIBUTORS

Srishti Publishers & Distributors
Registered Office: N-16, C.R. Park
New Delhi – 110 019
Corporate Office: 212A, Peacock Lane
Shahpur Jat, New Delhi – 110 049
editorial@srishtipublishers.com

First published by
Srishti Publishers & Distributors in 2020

10 9 8 7 6 5 4 3 2 1

This is a work of fiction. The characters, places, organisations and events described in this book are either a work of the author's imagination or have been used fictitiously. Any resemblance to people, living or dead, places, events, communities or organisations is purely coincidental.

Printed and bound in India

To my mothers.
Who have been, are and will always be the pillars of my strength and encouragement.

You are what you are,
So, if and when presented with the
Unexpected by life
One should learn from it and
Not run away.
Because,
The fight is always better than flight.

Acknowledgement

I thank the lord to have revived my passion for writing at the time when He knew I was going to be alone and clueless in life. He gave me my direction and a path of joy to follow.

I thank and appreciate my husband Vicky Kakar, and my children – Amandeep and Reet – for their love and for always being my support system.

Even though I had stunned everyone around me with the emergence of my first book *One Precious Moment,* they all were and are so proud of my achievement.

My family has – be it my husband, children, parents, in-laws, my sister, my brother, my sisters-in-law, niece, nephew – not only supported me, but continue to encourage me. Especially my husband (for whom I have now become Author Sahiba). More than me, they all want to see me achieve my heart's desires.

While I acknowledge all my loved ones for their love, support and encouragement, I need to especially thank my parents for making me the person I am, and my in-laws for always supporting me in doing whatever I wished to.

I most definitely wish to acknowledge my friend, advisor and the first person who helped edit my book *Love Unexpected* – Ms Mayura Amarkant. She not only helped draft my book into what it is, but helped me set the tone and pan out my book for submissions to publishing houses. Thank you Mayura, you are a true friend and a wonderful editor.

I would also like to thank Stuti and Arup for seeing potential in my story and helping me publish it. Team Srishti helped polish the diamond (that's what this book is for me) for the readers out there. Thank you again.

Last but not the least, I would like to thank the most important people – readers and book lovers. You are the reason we authors write, for whom stories are created. It is because of you lovely people that we love what we do. Thank you so much for helping us spread our passion and acknowledging our work. I say so with pride that my first book *One Precious Moment* was loved and appreciated because of you wonderful readers. Thank you very much for loving and reading books.

Heartfelt thanks to all my loved ones... friends and family and book lovers for your support, encouragement, care, love and most of all, your belief in me. It makes me confident that I will soon be able to reach that sky of mine.

1

Good lord! Who could be calling at this hour? Everyone knows better than to trouble me at work, especially from noon to 1:30 p.m., my busiest hours. The only time when the workload at the café is the least, thus the best time to sit and tally all the records, books, files and registers for my cafe. It's a chore that I hate to the core, but the final check has to be done by me. Being the boss has its downside, despite having an efficient staff. The phone continues to ring, I reach for it, to stop its grating sound.

Oops! It's Sam! We usually prefer to keep our conversations for home. No one knows better than him that I'm my worst enemy at this time of the day. So it has to be a good and valid reason. Hopefully not like the last time when he had called wanting to know *his* wife's favourite ice-cream flavour. Like seriously… he sure got a piece of my mind that day. Since then, today is the first time he has called.

"What!!??" I practically shout into the phone.

"OMG, OMG!!! What are you saying? For heaven's sake, slow down a bit. Begin again, and this time, go slow. Now tell me, how on earth is this possible? Like where? When? How?… No, forget that, please tell me is she okay? Why are you wasting your time calling me, you dork? You should be with her!" I shout in fear and panic.

The fear in my voice sure calms my brother a notch. When he speaks again, he uses the regular authoritative tone that he uses with me.

"Gosh Kaira, will you keep quiet, for heaven's sake? Your hyper attitude can create a ruckus enough to wake the dead. Damn it! You simply go on blabbering, making any normal conversations impossible."

I keep quiet for a few seconds only to snap back with twice the indignation.

"Hey, hey! If you back up a little, you will realise that a few seconds ago, you did not sound so cool yourself. In fact, you sounded possessed with fear and worry. So, don't try to act too smart with me; it is just the suddenness of the news that got me a little jittery."

After a small pause, I added sarcastically, "Sam, will you please settle down and talk. Your pacing around won't help you loose weight, but will sure give you and everyone around a headache."

"Oh god! Can you not crack jokes, especially at a time like this, sister dear? By the way, how did you know I was walking around?"

"Well, that is easy. You, dear brother, sound breathless. It usually happens when you are pacing around. So basically, you cannot even take small rounds without getting short of breath, huh!"

"Okay, fine! Now, stop listing my shortcomings and this meaningless rant. Please, just listen carefully. Tasha is fine. Yes, she is at the hospital, with the doctor attending to her as we speak. If all goes well, she will deliver our baby anytime soon. Kaira, I cannot express how thrilled I am! But her painful screams echoing through the entire ward is really making me nervous, and a little scared."

After a small pause, he whispers, almost sounding shocked at his words. "You know Kaira, I would never have believed Tasha could abuse if I had not heard it myself today. I mean, we have been together for more than four years now and she has never said such things. But man, it did sound sooo cool and hot coming from her."

A feeling of relief and calmness rushes through my nerves, and with it the need for answers surfaces. But hearing the last statement does bring a smile to my face. He sounds so zapped. If not for the seriousness of the situation, it would have been hilarious. So, I let it slide for now and start firing questions while gathering my stuff from the desk.

"But Sam, how? When? But mostly, why? Is it not a little too early? I mean, she is not due for another three weeks or so. So, what happened? And what are the doctors saying? How is the baby?"

He takes a deep breath and replies impatiently. I so detest this, but for now, I choose to focus on Tasha and the baby. I can imagine him waving his hand in the air as he attempts to explain the situation while continuing with his marathon across the hospital lobby.

"Her water bag broke while we were having lunch. As for your *why*... how the bloody hell should I know that? This is my first time too! Oh, goodness gracious, wait! I do know why. Yes, yes, actually my baby is super impatient just like her/his crazy aunt. Is that reason enough, eh?"

I let out a fake laugh and respond rather dramatically, "Yayayaa Sammy, I totally get it. You're really trying hard to be snarky, but you are awful at it, brother."

"Arrgh!! Kaira! Don't call me Sammy! You know I hate it. Especially now that I am going to be a father. It neither sounds mature, nor fatherly."

His breathing normalises, so I guess he has stopped walking. I can almost imagine him smiling slightly now.

I chuckle silently at having rattled him out of his sour mood. But I clear my throat before speaking again. If he as much as hears the humour in my voice, it would irritate him once again.

"Well, brother dear, that is a conversation for another time. Ohh btw! Why aren't you with Tasha? Why didn't you just ask mom to call?"

"I know! I too didn't want to leave Tasha alone right now. Calling you myself seemed easier and faster rather than going to look for mom. But now I wish I had, I would have returned to Tasha by now instead of the mindless chattering with you."

"Don't be mean, bro! You know I can't help questioning, and I love talking. Plus, when I left this morning, Tasha was absolutely fine."

"Yeah, okay, whatever! Now, I have no idea what difference your presence will make, but Tasha wants her bestie here. But for what it's worth, come quickly."

"Hey, that's not fair! You should know better than anyone what Tasha and my relationship means. So, my presence there is as significant as yours, brother dear."

"I know… I know! You know, hearing you go ballistic when I rattle you, especially about Tasha, gives me an amazing high."

"Hahaha! You are too funny Sammy! I understand you are stressed, but don't use me to calm your rattled nerves. Everything else aside, it's my right as an aunty to be with Tasha and you right now. I am, after all, your one and only sister, *the aunt!*"

"Gosh Kai! You are impossible! Now please get off your high horse and move it. Let's just pray that all goes well.

"Why are you stressing? You may be the cause of this situation, but I am the one who faced the flak. Remember all those checkups, sonographies, and boring pre-natal classes where I was forced to perform your role because you were busy!"

I imitate the obnoxious breathing noises taught in the classes just to pull another fast one on him. I speak in a low, poor me voice, "You know those classes were embarrassing and pretty torturous. But I did it, didn't I?"

I pause dramatically again, "But then you know what Sammy, this child is getting a lively, sexy, in fact the most amazing aunt ever! I am after all one of a kind! *The best!*"

I smile as I imagine the mixed feelings he must be experiencing right now.

"Will you stop self obsessing now and get on that stupid bike you own? We don't want another patient, so please ride carefully."

Before I can retaliate, he mutters, "Why can't you just get a car, like normal human beings?"

"You really are grumpy today! Actually, it is not that much of a surprise, huh. As for my bike and me, we are always careful. And FYI, cars are boring and take longer to reach places. Whereas my bike and I understand the roads and each other very well."

"Okay! Now, will you please hurry? Having to watch Tasha wither in pain was really difficult. Didn't know she was so strong… Come fast.. Kai."

Hearing his forlorn voice made my heart sink. "Hey Sammy! Chillax… Of course, she is strong. We women are made of steel when it comes to motherhood. Together, you will sail through this, like everything else you both have. Now, shush…!! Don't be a weak-hearted ass! Go in and take care of her as well as my niece/nephew till I arrive. Bye, I am OMW."

"Huh, what? What on earth is OMW?"

"What the f…!"

"Kairaaaa, please don't curse. Your slangs are incomprehensible. I just hate it when you talk like this."

"Okay, Mr Indignant, don't shout at me! I am twenty-five, not five years old. And you are twenty-eight, not eighty. Even though you act and behave like a senior citizen most of the time."

I sigh and exclaim, "Sam, you really need to start growing up and loosening up a bit. You are going to be a father now! And like seriously? You are asking what is 'omw'? It means 'On my way'. Even a kid knows that! It is so freaking common... ufff!! Okay, now stop talking so much! I really need to prep everyone here before leaving and you are delaying me. Plus, you need to be with your wifey, I will see you in a while. Bye! You take care now... see you soon."

I hurriedly hang up before he can start rambling again.

2

This is me. The *talker!* And where is the fun if you don't trouble your brother at every chance you get! In Sam's case, it is effortless to get a reaction from him. He is extreme when it comes to his emotions and attitude towards life. Being the oldest, he is very prim and proper too, all credit to his convent education.

He has a charming and caring side to him, but it's a latent one. A side one rarely gets to see. All this makes him an amazing and protective brother, making it tough for me to live up to his expectations.

Of course, all brothers are over-protective, especially when one has an impulsive nutcase like me as a sister. Yup! I know I am over-friendly and completely outspoken. My love for life and zest for the *now* is perpetual. I sometimes think that onlookers judge me as outrageous, but trust me, I am not so bad. After all, I run a Cafe Library with the help of a fantastic team, who are more like family. And where does it say café owners can't be mischievous and a tad bit crazy?

Shoot, I am doing it again, I need to speak to my team instead of daydreaming. I need to be omw like now, but I am going to be late (as usual).

I begin calling out to my team loudly, which makes everyone in the library look at me in sheer amazement! I was breaking my own rules. Oh god! I really am preoccupied to have broken my own golden rule.

As I start gathering my stuff, it occurs to me that Nikki will take my case for breaking the rules (shoot) as the library area is a complete silence zone.

My heart is beating loudly, pounding with excitement and joy. I am just dying to tell the world; I am going to be an aunt soon. But for now, it will be announced to the closest people in my circle.

"Nikita, Robin, Pete, guys please hurry! A quick word, I need to leave asap."

"Kaira, please don't bring down this place with your shouting. This is, after all, your Café Library, remember? So at least maintain the decorum of the place you created. Members are busy with serious work; you know that exam time is nearing for most students."

I reply hurriedly and nonchalantly, "Okay, okay, I am sorry. Now, where are the others?"

"Robin is at the bank to deposit this month's profits. Pete is helping Anita downstairs. It's a crazy day today. So, tell me, where is the fire?"

"Nikki baby, what will I ever do without you? You, my sweetheart, are the best accountant, manager and friend I have ever had… And no, there is no fire. I am going to become an aunt soon; Tasha is about to deliver the baby. So, you can understand my rush. I have to be at the hospital… like… *now*!"

"Oh, wow! Congratulations babes! How is Tasha doing?"

"Thank you! I don't know exactly how she is doing. Sam just called, and he sounded worried. I am rushing there and will update you. For now, you do me the honours and let the rest of the team know. Please, lock up the café as I will not be returning.

Before I leave, I want to make a small announcement. Could you switch on the mike for me please?"

"Okay! Listen up all my dear patrons slash friends slash book lovers, sorry for the rule break, won't happen again! Enjoy the first round of today's coffee on the house from the 'soon to be' aunt. So, all you lovely people, have fun!! You all know the rule - 'Silence is heaven for all'. All the best!"

I step away from the mike amidst huge cheering and shouts of congratulations from across the café. It feels amazing till Nikki interrupts my joy

"Kai, will you just leave? I will handle the rest. All the best and god bless!!"

"Darling!! I say this again and again… what will I do without you?"

"Survive! 'Cos that's who you are. But thank you for making me feel special and important."

"Hahaha, before this becomes an admiration society, I am leaving. Adios, amigo!!"

I stop midway and turn back… shoot! I am going to be even more late… but this was important…

"Oh god! I so forgot. Nikki! You remember I mentioned this new publishing company a few weeks back, 'The Lantern' and the owner Mr Aveer Mehra? The new face in the publishing market? The same guy who has made a huge name for himself in the recent years… do you remember him?"

"Yeah, I remember. He got nominated as the youngest entrepreneur in publishing. The name you went all gaga over, hmm? The man whose picture you searched the net, the papers and what not for."

She smiles mischievously. But I am too distracted and just shake my head in affirmation.

She asks in a professional tone when she sees my distracted look. "What about him?"

"He is bringing a new proposal for our café. I had mailed him a few weeks ago with a proposal to which he agreed. He is coming to negotiate for the range of international bestsellers, the new study material for students, magazines, etc. He says he had loved the concept of our Café Library and was impressed with its growing popularity. After a long discussion over emails, we agreed to meet today."

I look at my watch and then back at Nikki with a sigh.

"He is expected … like *now*!"

She knows exactly where this is going even as I give her my impish look, knowing it works every time.

"Will you please meet him? You know, to work out the basics. You can arrange for another appointment with me."

I pause to think of another date.

"How about day after tomorrow? Keep it for noon. That way you can update me on everything that is discussed today. For now, explain the reason for the change of plans. I'm sure he will understand."

Nikki's face has worry and concern written all over it, which surprises me, since she usually loves to tackle tough situations.

"But Kai… this is huge! You have been on it for some time now. What if I can't get it done? It will kill me to disappoint you. You have been very excited and hopeful about this venture. Why don't you just call him and postpone the meeting?"

"Don't talk like a stupid person! I know you can handle this like a pro, just like everything else you do. You know as much about the café as I do, if not more. It is not possible to postpone; he should be here any minute. I know you will nail it like you always do. Now bye. GTG."

Waving a bye, I rush down the stairs.

3

Shit, shit, shit, I am late!! I hurriedly dash down the long flight of stairs. Sam is going to kill me, and rightly so. Good heavens, how could I have forgotten about the meeting with Mr Mehra? I know Nikita will handle it but… Shoot!! Now, I will need to call him and explain. Gosh, why do I get stuck with organizing, updating, chatting, sorting… it causes unnecessary delay…. Hmm… I just can't help it, can I? I keep getting late. I really am going to start keeping that organizing diary, which everyone keeps telling me I need.

I am looking down and mumbling under my breath while rushing towards my scooty. Little do I know the unexpected turn of events that lay ahead.

As I rush down, I suddenly bang into a warm solid, muscular wall. Shoot! I should have seen where I was going. I find myself flying backwards as I feel the quick pull of gravity. A million thoughts race through my mind, the prominent one being the realization that my ass is going to hit mother earth soon and hurt in the next fifteen seconds. My hands are in the air, grasping for support. Alas! Despite all efforts, things are blurry and moving so fast all around me that I know my attempts to save my fall would fail.

My tote bag is now on the ground somewhere. I am cursing aloud without realizing I am doing so, while I try to break my fall. When all of a sudden, out of nowhere, I am pulled hard to safety by strong, warm and caring hands. He yanks me close, right against his chest.

I whimper, not realizing that it is actually audible, "Ufff! Oh, thank heavens! That was so bloody close."

I am breathless, struggling to gain control, but the warmth of his grip makes me want to hold on. His strength and masculinity are blowing my mind. My mind is working at the speed of light – 6 feet 1 inch tall. Nearly a foot taller than me, or so it seems, wow! Hmm, broad and toned shoulders with a very firm grip and a chest that has the capacity to bury all my angst. He just saved my ass, quite literally! But hey, that is bullshit! He is the cause of my downfall in the first place, huh! But wait… let me judge him later. While I breathe deeply to steady my nerves, his musky perfume hits my nose. Hmm, what smell is that… is it a touch of spice wood in his cologne? Wow, he smells really good! Does his face match these qualities?

I return from fantasy land. What on earth am I doing? Am I for real? My bestie is at the hospital, and I keep getting delayed. And now I am actually swooning over a stranger! Wow, god save me from my eccentricity. I don't have the time nor the luxury to acknowledge anything or anyone right now. Not even the impressive strength and scent of my saviour. I chuckle slyly to myself.

Maybe, if the time had been right, I might have enjoyed the moment. For now, I should just say a quick thank you for saving my ass, and just leave. Pulling myself away is an effort. Nonetheless, I slowly move my hands away from those amazingly broad muscular shoulders. But before I can so much as put in a word, Mr Strong Shoulders speaks, stunning me to silence (a very first) with his 'oh so sexy and so manly' voice.

"Hey, watch where you are going, lady! You need to curb that speed if you don't want to break your bones. You are lucky; I got you when I did."

WTF... Did this man just reprimand me? It's okay, isn't it? No! No one gets to do that! I was sooo going to be nice and thank him, but now no way on god's beautiful earth will he be getting that.

"Hey mister, *you* better watch it! If it weren't for you stopping suddenly, in the middle of the stairway, I would have sailed out. I mean… like… who freaking does that, huh? As you just said, I could have hurt myself badly. To top that, you pulled me so hard, I am lucky to have not dislocated a joint!"

"Okay, ma'am! Listen, you seem to be crying wolf here. I saved you from injury and didn't cause any harm. As for standing in the way, ma'am, you need to get your eyes checked. I am not standing in the middle of the stairway, Ms Fireball. You would have noticed this had you been careful, rather than flying out blindly."

"Ms Fireball? Like… really? How original!"

"Well, it suits you. After all, who argues with their saviour? Most people are thankful, but you are trying to make me feel guilty. As for the 'Fireball' analogy, well you do look like a ball of fire, all red and hot. And you are spitting fire."

He smiles and winks.

Did he just wink at me? Like, is this guy for real? Shoot! Screw him! I don't have the time for this, even though he is really hot… and his voice… oh man… it's giving me goosebumps… But right now, I need to leave, or else Sam and Tasha will kill me.

I know he was right. I should have thanked him, but now he can dream on. Had he given me a chance before opening his stupid but ohh so awesome mouth, he would have gotten his thank you and I would have left with happy memories and the thrill of having been saved by a handsome man. Well, his loss cause getting me to apologise now, that too voluntarily, is nearly impossible.

"You can say whatever you want. As for saving me, you did me no favours! It is your fault to begin with. Anyway, now move out of my way, I am getting late. I have no time for all this.Maybe some other time if you get that lucky. Toodle doo mister!"

I reprimand him with my index finger carelessly close to his face. Before he can utter another word, I rush out. But I do get a glimpse of him staring after me with surprise and wonder and a little fury in his eyes. It seems like no one has ever spoken to him like this. Well, what can I say, I am one of a kind!

But I have to mention that he is the hottest guy I have ever encountered. Looks which would get better with age, like good old wine which tastes better over the years. He must be in his early thirties, but that stubble makes him look rugged and really handsome.

He is dressed like he is a man who has money and power. His own boss, maybe. His eyes are a lovely shade of warm chocolate brown and they shine with arrogant intelligence. A proud, handsome man entering my café is worth my attention. But today is the wrong day.

Well, at this moment my priorities should be my family, not some attractive stranger. The saying, 'Que Sera, Sera' (whatever will be, will be) suits me right now. If ever we meet again, I would love to continue the sparring and enjoy admiring him. It has been a while since someone tickled my romantic side this way. I sigh to myself… yes… it has been long since…

Even as I rush towards my bike, I can still feel the heat of his eyes drilling into my back like lasers. I refuse to give him the satisfaction by looking back, as much as I want to. The need to see him one more time is overwhelming, but then it would have killed my dramatic exit. With a cheeky smile, I applaud myself for rendering him speechless as I drive away on my bike.

4

Well, well, well, you all are now wondering who this talker is. As you may know, I am Kaira… Kaira Kapoor. Kai to my friends and family.

Kaira means pure, whereas Kai means happy or ocean or loveable. Well, these names suit me because I am pure – pure fun and mischief. My friends know me as a joyful person filled with a zest for life.

As I wait for the light to turn green, I push my windblown hair back from my eyes. While I do this, I hear a loud whistle from the side-lines. I look up to see quite a good-looking guy eyeing me. Hmm… well, that makes me confident that I am not bad looking. My crowning glory is long, straight and silky brown. I am 5 feet 7 inches tall with brown eyes with a tinge of a champagne hue matching my hair perfectly. My complexion is more like caramel sauce mixed with a few drops of white chocolate sauce.

As the light turns green, I turn to the guy who is still eyeing me. I give him a cheeky smile and wave before going my way. I may be good to look at, but despite my attractive features, it is my bubbly nature which pulls people towards me. They say I have flawless skin, however, the mark above my eye disturbs me at times. Yes, I carelessly fell off my bicycle when I was around ten.

And then there is the second cut above my lip which I love. It is more like a war medal for me.

Wow, now this is one reason I love my bike. They call it Scooty, but I love calling it a bike. I get the freedom to think aloud without being seen as crazy. Now why is that mark a medal, huh, well it was from a battle I remember with glory and pride.

Shoot, the speed breaker! Ufff, that was a close save! I really need to watch where I am going, or else Sam's fears might come true.

Now, where was I just before my near fall at the speed breaker? Oh yes, about how my lip is scarred.

My bestie, Tasha and I reached for our first day in high school and some oversmart girls cornered Tasha. She was clearly not a fair pick to harass. Tasha was a meek introvert, who started hyperventilating when she was about to be ragged. I saw her while returning from the school office where I had to submit some papers. In retrospect, I could have handled the situation like an adult, but no, that is not me. I just have to act on impulse. So, I tighten my belt and jump in like Rani of Jhansi.

"Whoa girls! Why are you bullying someone who is no match for you? Look at her, she is shaking in fear, making you all look like idiots! Now, if you were fighting fair, with someone stronger, or at least more capable of handling you three, I would understand."

Wow, did I hit the beehive or what? It was terrific seeing the trio pull back their shoulders and stand erect. That sure was a 'ready to fight' pose! My comment had hit hard, shit! I looked around for a diversion, but seeing the crowd that had gathered, I knew it was war. Anyone who backed out now would look like a fool. It's just not in my DNA to back out. I quietly cursed myself for being impulsive, again. It was the first day of high school after all; none of us needed this.

Tasha tried pulling me back. I could hear her chiding me in a quivering voice, "God Kai, why can't you ever think before acting! It is our first day and you are already in a situation. Let's just leave."

Two of the bullies, our seniors (shit), were in my face, scowling at me. One of them said, "I think you should listen to your friend, newbie."

But then, she made the biggest mistake; she pushed me. Even Tasha who hardly ever curses, let out a string of abuse. Now there was no backing down; it was war. The girl who had pushed me soon found herself on the floor with me on top of her. The other two tried pulling me off, which led to hair pulling, a rain of blows, punches and slaps.

The crowd had a gala time at our expense. The college courtyard rang with whistles, cat calls, and humorous comments. We were unstoppable because it was now a matter of prestige and ego. Towards the end of the scuffle, two bullies had bruises and one had a black eye.

Whoopsie for me, ouch! I was not in good shape myself. I had a sprained wrist, scratches on my arms along with a sizeable upper lip cut, that needed stitches. And that, my friends, was the famous 'war medal / battle-mark' I am referring to.

Well, our drama caused quite a ruckus and the college management had to step in. We were pulled apart by some angry teachers who chided us for our childish behaviour. Imagine the first day of high school, and instead of sitting in class, we visited the principal's office!

I sigh happily as I remember that day. It was the most memorable day of my high school life, despite the firing and lectures or for my battle mark. My day of victory!

On the bright side, the clash of the titans broke the ice between us. With the trio, we formed our group that very first day. We were now the 'famous five'. They were a great support during the few years that we were together. In fact, we all are still in touch. Btw, their names are Maya, Pearl and Zoonie. Pearl and Maya are married and settled abroad. As for Zoonie, she now helps her dad in his business. I must call my girlies with the good news, or they will never forgive me.

Well, I can go on non-stop about my girlies, but my destination is finally here.

5

The best thing about bikes, you can find a place to park, asap. While parking, I remember the first time I met Tasha. Well, her name is Natasha Baig, but I think abbreviations are snappy and fun. Tasha and I met in the fifth grade when her dad got posted from Teheran to Mumbai. The fast pace, noise and the excitement that define this city was different from the Persian culture. She was used to a style of living that was quite opposite.

The oil company her father worked for, helped them in finding a home closest to work in a good locality. That's how we met. We were neighbours. While I was on the fourteenth floor, she lived on the sixth floor. As luck would have it, we were in the same school too.

Our first meeting was accidental and unexpected, but it bound us forever. We have been inseparable since then. We were in high school when I got my 'war medal scar'. In her I found a friend who is now more than a sister to me. She sure knows me better than anyone. Sometimes better than I know myself.

The sound of a blaring horn brings me back to my immediate surroundings, "Hey madam, look where you are going! There's no need to die under my car."

Shit, that is close again! Another bad habit of mine, 'daydreaming'. Whatever my faults, they were, are and will remain.

Tasha and my friendship has been strong for more than fifteen years now. Though now it is not just us. She cemented it by marrying my elder brother.

Huh! 'Love is blind'; whoever said that is damn right! But then, she could have been married to someone I may have hated, or he could have disliked me (it's not easy to like me, at least not instantly). Then what would have happened? OMG! That is scary to even imagine! I would rather be talking about her sex life with my brother than not have her in my life at all. Though it is a disgusting conversational choice, he is my elder brother after all. Now to add to this circle of love, we have a baby on its way.

Here I am, at the hospital. Thankfully without broken bones, nor any other mishaps. Wonders never cease to happen. I reach my destination in one piece with no more arguments. I rush to the nurse station to enquire when I see Sam pacing the floor. I look around for mom, but there is only him with a look that scares me. I rush to him and start off without pause, as usual.

"What the hell are you doing here? Why are you not with Tasha? Now is not the time to have cold feet. Is she okay? Where is mom? What are you looking at? Say something, for heaven's sake!"

"If you stop your rambling for once, only then will I be able to tell you anything."

"Ya, okay. I am sorry, but seeing you all gloomy and pacing around like this got me scared. She is okay, na?

"Yes, or at least I think so. They are doing a C-section right now, as we speak."

"What the fuck… why? She was doing fine. All the tests and ultrasounds were perfect. The doctor said she was doing well. So, what's wrong?"

For once he does not scold me for cursing, which just shows how worried he is. And I speak a full sentence instead of my abbreviation, like I always do, huh. This is serious!

"Kai, stop getting worked up. The doctor told me all is fine. It is just that the umbilical cord got wrapped around the baby's neck. They tried everything to avoid the operation, but it wasn't possible. Which is why they rushed her to the OT."

I can feel the increased rate of my heartbeat and goose bumps all over my body as I speak,

"Why didn't you mention this to me when you called earlier?"

"All was going well then. This complication occurred after our conversation. I think the baby turned or something like that."

"Shit, shit, shit, have you called her family. And where is mom?"

"Yes, her parents are on their way. As for mom, she is praying in the lounge. You better go to her. She has been crying ever since they took her in. She needs your positive dose."

I give him a quick hug and rush to where mom is. When I see him put his hands in his hair in frustration and worry, I stop and call out, hoping to irritate him into easing a little.

"Hey Sammy, don't worry, both will be fine. After all, I am going to be the one to hold him first."

It is another sign of how worried he is, because he gives me a lame smile. Typically, he would have started a squabble with me. I quietly turn away. Just as I am about to switch to the corridor, I hear my name.

"Kaira..."

"Uhh... ya!!"

"You know we all need your positivity right now. You are the only one among us all who stays calm in the face of problems. So, spread the brightness."

"Hey, do not go all mushy on me, brother dear. Btw, you know I hate it when you call me Kaira. It's stopping me from talking BS with you and turn respectful."

I give him a flying kiss and thumbs up. Before I turn, I shout back, "Hey Sammy, before you ask again what btw and BS mean…"

"By the way, I know, and as for BS, I know that too. I don't have to expand on it to encourage your nonsense."

"Good going bro, you are learning. I am impressed!"

I smugly smile at him and go in search of my mother, all the while praying for both Tasha and junior.

While I am as scared and worried, I need to be strong to support the family.

We are in the best nursing home, with the best doctors. This may be a small place, but the care and facilities here are beyond excellent.

The atmosphere around is homely and bright. It is not like a regular hospital where everything from the walls to the doors to the curtains are white. The air smells fresh and flowery, not like the terrible medicine-infused air at other clinics and hospitals.

I reach the lounge, where I find mom curled up in a chair. Tears are running down her cheeks. Luckily, it's just us in here, giving us privacy. Only the father is allowed anywhere near the OT or the lobby. I give Mom a tight hug and she breaks into sobs.

"She is going to be OK, Mom! You have told us a million times that it is natural. Every woman experiences it once in her life. So why are you crying? You have brought two into this world. Tasha will do so too!"

"I know Kai. It's just that saying and seeing is different. Especially now, as she is being operated."

I hug her again. Being in her arms reassured my fearful soul. "Mom, it's going to be fine. You don't have to worry. She is strong, and so is our baby."

I hold her hand tight in support; she has been a mother to both Tasha and me forever. So, when Sam and she fell in love, mom was the happiest of all. She is one of the gentlest persons I have ever seen. Extremely patient, especially with crazy children like us. We gave mom some tough times, but she handled everything with love, care and a smile. I cannot recall a time when she shouted or raised a hand on us.

Mom was the first person to whom Sammy and Tasha confessed their love. Even though Mala aunty was not against it, Tasha was afraid to speak to her about it. She too knew that Mala aunty was bound by her husband's rules and assertive nature. So, mom was a safe choice to keep a secret.

"Hey Mom, remember when Sammy had come with Tasha to you? God, I still can't get over the look on your face. You were expecting it, despite us trying to keep it under wraps, waiting for our finals to complete before speaking to you all. If Baig uncle had not thrown in the shocking news of Tasha's possible marriage, we would have kept quite a little longer."

"Of course, I remember. You are right; I was expecting it. Mala and I had already spoken about it, so we were not surprised. You children think you all are smart, but you all tend to forget that we are your parents."

"You had actually had a conversation with Tasha's mom about it?! Like really? Wow! She never said anything about it!"

"Well, even though Mala understood Tasha's reasons, still she was a little hurt by it. Later, it was water under the bridge and she did not want to make Tasha feel guilty. So, you better not repeat this to her."

"Ya ya, even I would not want to upset them. Mala aunty is too sweet, and all this is history now."

I get up while talking to mom to check if Sam is around with an update. When I don't see him out in the corridor, I walk back.

God! What is taking so long? The C-section should be done by now. I start pacing the floor.

I stop by the window watching the heat of the sun draining as the evening approaches. It's nearly four hours since Sam's call.

"Mom, tell me something! How did you get Baig uncle's agreement? I was sure he would say no. I mean, he's always been set in his Islamic outlooks. I mean, he had a guy in mind for Tasha, so..."

I say with dramatic effect, "What is the secret behind that?"

"It's no secret sweetheart! When the question is about your child's happiness, every parent wants the best. At such a time, every parent only sees who will make his child happy? Or how secure she will be? Or how the family of the boy is? Will they love his daughter, take care of her? Mr Baig did not have to think twice when Mala approached him. He knew it was the perfect match, knowing Samarth and us. So, we were sure he would not object."

It's so amazing how parents always know. We are the fools who try being smart and independent. When the fact is, we will still be children and never more intelligent or more knowledgeable than them.

I look back at mom and see the memories shining in her eyes. I too get lost in them.

On the reception day, Baig uncle got a little drunk and went up to the podium and gave a thank you speech. Wow, it was a sight to behold! In all these years, we never had heard him speak more than a few words. He usually greeted us or enquired briefly about our exams.

I was a bit intimidated by him and never had the guts to open my mouth in front of him. I don't even fear dad, who can be super scary when annoyed, but that is so rare that I tend to forget.

"Hey, mom. What are you thinking?"

"The same thing as you, since you mentioned Mr Baig. It really was a sweet speech."

Both mom and I look at each other and smile.

"Dear friends and family, thank you all for your presence here today and for all your best wishes."

The reception hall had suddenly fallen silent. Even Mala aunty had a stunned expression as she watched her husband adjusting his tie while addressing the crowd. I went to stand by Tasha, in case she needed me. We exchanged surprised and worried looks, wondering what he was going to say.

"Now, I could have had a long line of eligible bachelors for my beautiful daughter. In fact, I did have a boy in mind. He was richer and slightly more handsome than Sam. No offense to you son!"

We all started laughing. Even the sensitive Sam let out a loud, nervous laugh. He surprised us by calling out, "None taken, Dad."

Tasha's eyes welled up in tears. Sam had not called her father 'Dad' till now. Even my parents were happy.

Uncle continued, "But one thing that I could never have guaranteed her with the other boy was the surety that he was a good human being. I could never be sure if he would be a good husband, nor someone I could trust to love Natasha more than me. But my daughter herself chose, not a son-in-law, but a son for me. So, instead of her saying anything to me, I am going to say a thank you to her for choosing such a wonderful life partner and the perfect family."

Hearing these beautiful words from a man who never said anything brought tears of joy to everyone's eyes. It was an emotional moment watching Tasha go up to uncle and hug him tight. It must have been the first time for all, watching them embrace. Much as uncle loves Tasha, he never shows it. We had always seen him very quiet and ever watchful. So, to watch him cry while he held Tasha was the most amazing moment.

While mom and I are holding hands remembering those awesome moments, Sam rushes into the room. Seeing his smiling face and the joy in his eyes bring relief and happiness. I rush to him just about to ask when he shouts, "It's a girl! We have a beautiful, totally gorgeous angel in our family!"

Mom hugs him tight, and I jump in joy.

"Hey Sam, how is Tasha?"

"She is also fine. Tired due to the prolonged operation. But the doctor said she is doing good."

Wow, I look around the room which suddenly seems brighter. We now have reason for another celebration. More joy and happiness to grace our house. I am just about to start clapping when the door opens to let in Mala aunty.

6

Amidst all the hugging and crying, the imp in me makes me climb on the table.

"Attention! Attention! Please! Heartiest congratulations to grandma Kapoor and grandma Baig for the newest addition in the family. Btw, where are the grandfathers?"

My announcement brings a pause to all the hustle. When Sam sees me on the table, he slaps his forehead.

"Kai, for heaven's sake, get down! You are no longer the baby of the family! We have someone smaller who has taken that position. You need to behave like a mature aunt now. So, how about you start to grow up now?"

"Oh, sure Daddy! I will start practicing from tomorrow. So, till then I can be the baby, right?"

Everyone starts laughing seeing my expressions. I contour my lips downward and make a baby face. I jump down the table and go to the others.

"Okay, now when can we meet the mother and child, brother dear?"

"They are finishing with the stitches and cleaning the baby right now. The nurse said it should be another half an hour before they shift them to the room."

"Oh cool, let me call the grandfathers and give the good news. They should have been here long back."

I look at everyone waiting for an answer. But suddenly there is a deafening silence in the room. What… is going on here? I put my hand on my waist and look at mom,

"Okay, what on earth are you all hiding from me? Where are the grandfathers? Everything is kk no?"

I see both moms look at each other. I cannot fathom the conversation between their eyes. But a few seconds later, mom shakes her head in negative. I am just about to jump in again with questions when Sam calls his mother-in-law.

"Mamma, I think we should go check on Tasha!"

Okay, now I know something is cooking for sure. Sam's attempt to leave mom and me alone is weird. The minute the door to the lounge closes I turn to mom.

"Sam really needs to brush his tactics. He is way too obvious. So now that it's just us, are you going to tell me what is going on?"

I hear mom sigh, which is surprising. She is always so ready to handle any situation. I think Tasha's sudden trip to the OT has shaken her more than she is showing. I move slowly to her side and put my arm around her shoulder.

"Mom, I am sure it can't be that bad. I mean, if you have to weigh your words before you speak means something is not right. You know I can handle anything with you by my side, so just get it over with."

"Sweetheart, I am sorry. I know I should have mentioned this earlier, but with Tasha's delivery and then all the reminiscing, it slipped my mind."

And then she goes quiet again. Wow, that is so not her!

"Okay, mom, dramatics are only for one person in this house, *me!* You are making me nervous. Will you just speak now?"

"Okay Kai, dad has gone with Mr Baig to the airport, to pick Drew."

"Whaaat? Drew is coming? When did this happen? How come dad has gone with uncle?"

"Sweetheart, Mr Baig had told Drew that Tasha is due soon, so if he wanted to come, he would be welcomed. Mr Baig consulted with us before making the call. He did not want any of us upset with Drew's presence. We assured him on your behalf as well that it would be fine. After all, sweetheart, it's been four years since the incident."

I start pacing the lounge and mindlessly fiddle with my hair while thinking of how to handle this news. I know what she is saying makes sense. But I just am not ready to face my biggest mistake, and trust me, I make many. Seeing me pace frantically, mom shouts my name, bringing me to a standstill. Mom never shouts. Wow, she sure is wound up!

"Kai, will you stop pacing like this? Listen, Drew has tried a million times to apologize for something you both were at fault for. He has even tried to get his father to forgive him, but for your sake, Mr Baig hasn't forgiven him yet. We all forgave you and your immature act, but he is still paying."

I look at mom with shame and hurt in my eyes. I know she has never said it, but she is very hurt and humiliated with my past behaviour. I turn to the window seeing the sky change colour as the night approaches. It is an amazing sunset which I would generally have appreciated, but at this point, tears are blinding me. I blink fast to stop the drops from falling. I don't want mom to see the tears, nor guess how upset I am.

"Kai, your dad and I believe that this would be a perfect time to forgive and forget the past. I say this especially keeping Mala in mind. Her son has been away from her for too long now. He has paid the price for something, I repeat, where you too were equally at fault."

"Okay, you don't have to keep saying that. I know I was guilty, but I did not know nor expect the outcome. But I agree with you, it is time to stop this cold war. I know he is Tasha's brother and deserves to be here at a time like this."

Mom hugs me quietly. I know she can feel my pain. Even though four years have passed, I cannot forget the hurt and humiliation that scarred me forever.

"Hey, now just because I agree doesn't mean that I am ready to forget everything that happened. I understand that Drew should be back with his family. Just don't expect me to be friendly with him. I will be nice, but I would rather be miles away from him."

"Good girl! You make me proud with your maturity. This is a special time for all of us, so let us all just start over. And I'm sure time has changed him too. After all, there have been changes in your nature and outlook in these four years."

"What changes mom? I am the same, just stronger."

"Sweetheart, just sometime back I told you that I am your mom. You can try, but not hide from me."

"Okay, whatever. I think we have talked for way too long. You have warned me, or should I say prepared me. Now, let's go and see the new baby of the house."

As I am about to open the door, she hugs me again. I know she can see how apprehensive I am about Drew's coming, but as she said, we need to move ahead and not remain in the past. Though I can't help the shiver that runs through me at the thought of seeing him again. Four years have passed since I last saw him. Under circumstances that I don't want to think of ever. Well, one doesn't always get what one wishes, do they?

I walk behind mom quietly, my mind distracted. The excitement of being an aunt is subdued with this new development. Drew, a name I had buried deep down, is now in my face.

Drew is not even his given name, but a shortened version of Drewster. Drew's name sounded more like a rooster. He changed it because of the ruthless teasing at school. Out of nowhere, he declared himself as Drew one day. Seeing how adamant he was; even uncle made it official.

I am so deep in my thoughts that I don't see the man standing in front of me, watching me. I just walk straight into him, losing my balance for the second time today. I am falling back when I feel arms go around my waist stopping my fall. I sure have been lucky today. Twice my backside has been saved from meeting mother earth. But they say luck doesn't always favour you. As I look up to thank the stranger, I stop in shock. The stranger is not unfamiliar. I don't even realize that I whispered his name.

"Drew..."

"Hi, Kaira. How are you?"

His casual question leaves me a bit stunned. Usually, I would reply as casually, but seeing him shut my brain. I am trying to come up with a response when I realize his hands are still on my waist. I pull myself back with a suddenness that nearly makes me loose my balance again. But fortunately, luck has not left me totally. I manage to regain balance.

I look up to him and feel a dart of pain deep within. He has not changed much.

Those sharp, beady, black eyes were like lasers which could always look right through me. His hair that once used to fall on his forehead, especially that one tress which I used to love playing with, was now all gelled and swept back. His style of dressing and his appearance had changed. Earlier, it was only jeans and t-shirts that is now replaced with trousers and a cotton shirt. He sure is as handsome as ever, more so. But just not someone I now want to associate with any more than needed.

7

I reach out to the depths of my brain to bring out the strong and confident Kaira. The one who promised herself that nothing would ever bring her down ever again. As soon as I find her, I look straight into Drew's eyes and reply curtly, "Hi, Drew. I am doing good. You look good. How are you?"

He is surprised by the normalcy of my tone. I don't think he was expecting this reaction from me. I give him my most confident look while he examines my face carefully like a nervous child now.

"I too am doing good. Busy with the hectic pace there, but now kind of used to it. How ab…."

He was going to talk more but luckily the moment gets shattered with the sound of someone arguing. We turn to see Sam arguing with the nurse. I rush to him, not bothering to see if Drew followed.

"Sam, Sam! What is it?"

"It's been thrity minutes now, and they are still not letting me see Tasha. As for my angel, they just showed me a glimpse of her and then nothing."

I pull him away from the nurse, apologizing for his behaviour. I take him to the corner.

"Sam, chillax, will you? Remember, you are the cool and collected one. This is a hospital, and they are doing their job.

Listen, why don't you go to mom while I find out what's causing the delay."

"Okay, but come back soon. I am getting a very weird feeling."

"I will be back asap, K?"

I must have hardly taken a few steps towards the nurse station when Sam stops me again

"Hey Kai…"

I turn thinking he had something important to say but noooo!!

"Was that Drew you were talking to?"

Like seriously, despite the chaos he is creating, he has the time to notice who I was with? Wow! He really is an amazing but crazy brother! Instead of answering him, I walk away.

"Hello sister… please, could you give me an update on Natasha Kapoor? She just delivered a baby girl."

"Ma'am, I just told her husband that we are getting the room ready. As for the baby, well she is with the doctor in the nursery. Ma'am, you need to understand that these things take time. Cleaning the mother, changing her clothes, bathing the baby and checking vitals, it all takes a while."

"Well, when you put it like that, I understand. It is just that it has been long. We all are getting impatient. Please let us know when Tasha is in the room."

"Of course, ma'am."

"Thank you."

As I turn, I bang into Drew who is standing right behind me. I move to the side, avoiding any more contact. I mutter an "Excuse me" while I walk towards Sam. Once again, he speaks, "You have changed Kai."

I turn around, startled hearing my name from him after so many years. I look at him questioningly,

"Huh?!!"

"I mean, you have mellowed down. The Kai I remember would have been arguing and trying to get inside the OT, if need be. But the one I see in front of me very calmly accepted the nurse's word."

"Who said I am calm? And who says I won't be trying to see Tasha before everyone?"

I give him a sweet but a totally mischievous smile and go to Sam.

"Brother dear, she is still in the recuperating room outside the OT. Should be another ten minutes max."

"Okay. By the way, what was Drew saying?"

"Like really Sammy. Chillax, please. Don't give me a headache about this. Especially when you did not warn me before today. You knew, didn't you?"

Sam avoids my gaze as I leave him standing in the hospital corridor. Now, no one would have guessed my destination. I walk confidently towards the recovery room, making sure no one is watching.

I stop outside the door where Tasha could be. I look around once to make sure no one is there to stop me. I can see two nurses talking with their backs towards me, so taking advantage of the opportunity, I peep in. When I see Tasha alone in the room, I sigh in relief. I slowly tip toe towards her, making sure she isn't disturbed.

She looks pale and drained out. The colour of her skin matches the sheets that are covering her. She is missing the usual reddish glow on her cheeks, a gift of Persian blood. In fact, the entire Baig family is fair-skinned with apple red cheeks and black soulful eyes. As I softly caress her forehead, she opens her eyes.

I find myself staring lovingly into a familiar pair of eyes. However, this time, the look brings tears of happiness to mine.

They look tired, but happy. I kiss her on her forehead and exclaim, "Hey, Mommy dear! Congratulations!"

"Hey, aunty dear! Congratulations to you too…"

She gives me a weak smile and looks around the room. I guess she was looking for the rest of the family. She feebly remarks, "They haven't shifted me yet! This is the restricted zone. How did you land in here?"

"Ya babes, it is. But then you know me, waiting isn't made for me. Also, Sam is getting worried and stressing everyone out there. Most importantly, how can anyone else meet you before me?" I wink at her as she smiles back. I continue speaking. "Sam got lucky with angel because mom had me cornered. But with you, I had to check first, that too personally."

She chuckles and exclaims, "God Kai…!! Now that you have seen me, *go!* I don't want you to get into any trouble with the authorities here."

She stares at the door as if an army is going to barge in any moment. Her agitated look tells me that I shouldn't be arguing with her. She is in pain after all.

"Okay, I am going. Don't stress! You may be weak, but from the way you are ordering me around, I can say you are fine. Thank god for that! Bye, see you soon mommy!"

I turn to leave after giving her a warm hug. Just as my hand moves towards the door handle, a nurse barges into the room. OMG! I feel my heart begin racing and getting ready for a confrontation, but god saves me yet again. The door covers me partially, and she is in such a hurry that she walks past me without noticing. I take this opportunity and rush out to the family.

As I walk back, my lips break into a happy smile. Tasha is fine, the baby is fine and I am one happy aunt!

"So, you have not changed. Just become smarter."

I let out a short yelp as Drew calls out.

"Shit! Don't do that! I could have had a heart attack! Ya... well... I just wanted to make sure she was genuinely kk. After all, it has been a while since we are waiting."

I keep walking, not wanting to pursue the conversation any further. I look up to see Sam eyeing us suspiciously. I sigh, shrug my shoulders in exasperation and continue walking.

"Well, an update. Tasha is doing good, tired but fine. They are just wheeling her to the room. So, we should be called in anytime now."

"How do you know this?"

"God Sammy! I went in and met her. How else will I be able to tell?"

"Kaira, will you stop calling me Sammy? And how did you enter the OT?"

I sigh again, his constant questioning is irritating me. Now would not be the place or time to start an argument. My good lord knows, Sam can test the patience of a saint, and I am no saint! What is pissing off is that even dad never questions me so much. I open my mouth to ask mom why she isn't saying anything to him and just then, the nurse calls out to Sam. Thank god, today has sure been a dramatic day for me.

8

"Hurray! Saved by the nurse. Now, how about we go in to meet the mommy and baby? What say Sammy, that is more important, huh?"

I hear a chuckle behind, but don't turn to look. I know it is Drew. One more word from Sam and I would lose it for sure.

Maybe if he holds his baby, he will forget about admonishing me. Drew is standing near the wall with his hands folded to his chest, enjoying the show. Still an a'hole! Gosh!

Mom must have noticed the possibility of Sam losing it totally now, so she finally intervenes, "Okay children, let us go. They won't give us much time with Tasha and the baby. Later, only a couple of us can stay with her."

Sam darts me an irritated look before he leaves grumbling all the way. The atmosphere changes instantly as we follow him. There is excitement and a spring to everyone's feet. One could almost hear everyone's heart beating with happiness, especially the mothers who pick up speed nearing the room.

The room we enter is like the rest of the hospital. Bright, warm, very homely. The walls are a shade of pink with cute caricatures adorning them. The décor possesses the power to make even the most unwell person feel calm and happy.

Tasha is propped up with a few pillows. She looks happy to be surrounded by family.

The moms are flanking her, one is caressing her forehead and the other is playing with her hair. Sam is at her feet while Drew stands by the door watching everyone. Once again, I realize that the grandfathers are still not around. With Drew here shouldn't they also be here? I hurriedly exclaim,

"Hey, where are the grandfathers now?"

"Gosh Kai! Could you please tone it down a little?"

"Oh! Sorry… but it just struck me that they are still not here."

"Well, if you had not gone for your 'see Tasha first' mission you would have met them. They have now gone to the nursery to see Angel."

"Angel?? We named her already?? When???"

"Since no name has been decided, she shall be Angel till then."

"Aye aye captain!"

Both mothers shake their heads while we continue squabbling. But then both of us just cannot help it. Sam and I look at each other with gleaming eyes, thinking this is and will always be us.

The door opens and the nurse is carrying our bundle of joy. I rush to get her, but my dad who was right behind the nurse makes it before me. I wail loudly, "Dad! That's not fair. You got to see her first. At least let me hold her."

I put my arms out in the hope that he would place Angel in them. But before he could even think of it, mom takes her from dad! Angel coos happily, as if she is enjoying the game.

"Heeyy!!! Wt…?" Before I can complete, my brother and dad chide me loudly,

"Kai!!!"

"Kai watch it, there is a baby in the room now."

In his classic intrusive style, Sam adds, "Even if she wasn't, there are parents here. At least show some respect!"

I slap my forehead. I am totally fed up of this man.

"Sammy, firstly I was using abbreviations. Secondly, Angel is too young to even understand what I say. And lastly, dear grandpa, our parents are used to my codes to be offended anymore."

I sigh and look around

"Oh, btw another thing, look around you. No one is interested in what we say. So, take a chill pill. Your straight-jacketed attitude will give you pain in your back someday."

"Ufff, Kai!! What should I do with you?"

"For now, just get me Angel from the grandparents. They seem to think they are the only ones promoted here."

Sam looks over to the bed and smiles happily. I look at Sam and can't resist needling him again.

"Well, one good thing has happened today. I am finally free from your dictatorship. From now on, my niece is going to keep you occupied and be under your watchful eyes."

"Hahaha, how you wish it were true! You are the baby of this house and will always remain that. You are and always will be my responsibility… at least until we find someone as crazy as you who is ready to take over my job."

"Ya right, you wish!"

My god, what is it with brothers, especially elder brothers? Why do they feel they need to be protective all the time? Well, I know Angel will keep him occupied for me.

A new family member, a new beginning, a new chapter in life. Life at every step brings new challenges, dreams and situations to face. This is ours, my niece, our joy and hope; rest can be handled as it comes.

Seeing that I won't be getting a chance to hold my niece anytime soon, I take this opportunity to call the Café. It is nearly closing time and everyone would be wrapping up. As I wait for someone to answer the phone, my mind wanders, reminiscing about the events of the day. My mind drifts back to the handsome stranger. I can still picture him standing there, looking arrogantly at me. The surprised look in his brown eyes at my cheekiness. The spark of indignation making his eyes a warm shade of caramel... Wow!

As a shiver runs through me when I think of his booming, aristocratic voice, the loud crackling voice on the phone in my hand breaks the train of my thoughts, "Hello! Anyone there?"

"Yaya, I am there! Nikki, I mean I am here. Sorry I got lost in thoughts."

"Oh, Kaira it's you!! I have been hollering for a while and was just about to disconnect. Anyway, how is everything there? Has Tasha delivered?"

"Yes, she has. We have a beautiful angel among us now."

I hear Nikki scream in joy and call the rest of the members. I can hear chairs being dragged and the vacuum cleaner going off. I can visualize everyone rushing to Nikki. She puts the phone on speaker and they all sing the congratulations song while clapping loudly.

Their love and happiness overwhelm me. It takes love and understanding to have good relations with anyone. I am blessed to have not only found the perfect work team, but friends among them. They have stood by me and nurtured the Café for nearly three-and-a-half years. Without them, life will always be incomplete now.

"Thank you, thank you, thank you, friends. Congratulations to you all as well. Now, how was the day at the Café?"

OMG! I think I touch a nerve there! All of them start speaking at once, each with their own version of how the day had progressed without me.

"An author had booked for a reading session, to top that there were more customers than normal. It was an exhausting day."

"There was a never-ending line at the bank today. The place was a sauna as the AC was not working."

"Shucks! Don't talk about today! I told you to postpone the meeting, but do you ever listen? No! For the first time I got to deal with a man as bad as you. In fact, worse."

Nikki is the most organized and sorted person among us. She has the brain of a finance wizard, intelligence of a genius and a calm personality. She keeps all of us in line. To hear her hassled and agitated tone means something big happened to ruffle Miss Cool's feathers.

"Ohkay, what happened?"

The second I ask the question, the others bid me bye and leave. Nikki takes a deep breath as she takes the phone off the speaker to narrate her experience.

"Okay, your Mr Aveer, the 'brave one' is arrogant, rude and an absolute devil. That arrogant asshole of a devil treated me like mere staff, something you have never made any one of us feel like."

"Woah! What did he say? And why? Did you not explain who you were? And what's with the 'brave one' jab?"

She continues breathing heavily. Wait, is she crying?

"It's the meaning of his name, silly! I cordially greeted him and offered him coffee while I explained your sudden rush to the hospital. I explained that I was authorized to conduct the meeting and discuss the proposal on your behalf. But midway through my explanation, the condescending ass stood up and started berating. He was extremely mean and hurtful."

She clears her throat among her sniffles and then continues. It takes me a second to realize that she is imitating him.

"Ma'am, I am sure you are smart and intelligent. I am also sure you can handle anything, even this meeting. But you are not the owner of this Café Library, whom I was to meet. If she had a crisis, she should have had the decency to call and reschedule the meeting and not let someone else handle it, however capable."

She pauses for a second. I am about to say something, when she just starts again.

"I am taking your leave, ma'am. You can let your boss know that if she wishes to do business, then she must be present for the next meeting. Or else I will assume she's not interested."

I hear her clear her throat again, she gulps loudly. I guess she was sipping water. But this time, before she can say anything, I jump in.

"Oh god Nikki! I am so sorry, that must have been tough. Was he really that arrogant or are you making it up?"

She scoffs and exclaims, "Really Kai? Do you really think I would make a joke about something this important? Trust me, he was the devil in a Prada suit."

"Woooow, a Prada! Rich dude, huh?"

Hearing her screech, I push the phone away from my ear.

"All you could gather was the Prada suit? I was being sarcastic, woman! How would I know if it was a Prada?"

"Oh!!"

She scoffs once again at my reaction. She seems really outraged and hurt. I turn serious and stop being a bitch.

"Okay, look, I am sorry! That was a poor joke. Well, now we know Aveer is rude and a devil, so we will deal with him accordingly. Did you set up another appointment with the Devil in Prada?"

"Oh heavens, Kai your sense of humor is cryptic and badly timed. Here I am explaining that I did not get to talk business and you are making fun of me!"

"Don't worry Nikki. I will deal with the man and his condescending attitude when I meet him. However, till then I have the right to find humour in the situation. Why take stress about something we cannot change at present, huh?"

"Yes, I understand... you and your positive outlook towards situations. As always, you are right. Nothing can be done about him right now. And yes, I did manage to set up an appointment for the day after tomorrow, 12.30 p.m., as you had said."

She lets out a sigh, letting me know she is getting late. The fact that I have been out here longer than expected makes me end the call with an abrupt, "Okay, listen I have gtg. I still haven't held Angel. Okay, bye."

I hang up abruptly, without waiting to hear her goodbye. The conversation with Nikki is still running through my mind as I enter the room. We have been working for more than three years, but Nikita has never written off anyone like this, nor been this flustered. There has to be more. For now, I shift my focus to the present; it's time for celebrations! The rest can wait.

9

I open the room to the sound of Angel crying. The atmosphere is resonating with love and joy. Everyone was beaming, even Drew. Everyone has had their share of cuddling with Angel, and it is my turn now. Before cuddling Angel, I rush to Tasha to give her a warm hug.

She appeared upset, "Where have you been for the past twenty minutes? I thought you would be more excited…"

Wow! Post-delivery not only makes mothers weak and exhausted, but whiners as well! But she is right, the work could have waited. I touch both my ears, apologetically.

"I am sorry mommy! I know I should have stuck around for my turn. I just felt it would be better to let everyone get over their excitement first. Later it would be just the three of us anyway…"

Everyone in the room made booing sounds at my logic.

"Hey family, you are supposed to support me, not cause ripples! Can't you see that she is annoyed?"

"Shut up Kai! You and your melodrama! Now do I get that hug or not?"

I hug her tightly and kiss her on the forehead before turning for Angel. I quickly pull back my stretched hands when I realize that Angel is in Drew's arms. Now, this is awkward. Having Drew around is kk, but to actually come in physical contact with him is not on the cards.

My mind begins to strategize ways of taking Angel from him, when Tasha's mom brings her to me. Except for Drew, no one realized how effortlessly she helped avoid any awkwardness at this special moment. She sure is a wonderful lady, one who would have been a wonderful mother-in-law, but alas, such is life…!

The moment Angel is in my arms, I forget everything else. She is the cutest and the most beautiful baby I have ever seen! Upturned nose, beady eyes and soft skin. The shape of her face is like Sam's, but the skin colour and the features, even the chin are undoubtedly like Tasha.

As I caress her cheek, I absent-mindedly exclaim, "OMG, I would never have guessed that Sam could have created such a gorgeous baby!"

I don't realize that I speak aloud until the whole room bursts out in laughter. Sam, of course, scoffs in annoyance; he has every right to.

I turn red in the face and look up. Shit, all eyes are on me!

"Oops, I am sorry! Before anyone says anything. I admit that is careless and a little mean…but don't you all agree that it's true?"

I smile slyly and dart a look towards Sam. He is smiling!

"Today you can say anything you want, baby sister. I am too happy to get upset with you."

"Okay people, jokes aside, how about thinking of a perfect name for Angel? Since all of us are here, we can think of a nice one. I seriously refuse to call her Sweetie, Pumpkin, Chiku, blah blah blah. So, mommy, daddy, what names do you have in mind?"

"Well, it is also an aunt's prerogative to choose. So, do you have a name in mind?"

"Well, I do have two names. Tasha, do you remember we discussed them? 'Aira' means the beginning or breath of life and the other is 'Arshi' meaning the first rays of the sun or a queen. I think you liked one of these and wanted to discuss it with Sam. Which one was it?"

While the question hangs in the air, Angel starts crying loudly. The nurse enters the room with a tray, sets it aside to take the baby from me. I am so not ready to let go of my bundle of joy, but her needs come first. As the nurse takes Angel from me, she asks everyone to leave.

The grandfathers leave quickly. Sam kisses Tasha goodbye and follows Drew out, leaving the grandmothers and me in the room. I look at mom imploringly, she replies, "No, Kai you cannot stay with her. She needs assistance with the baby. You wouldn't know what to do. I am going to request the doctor to allow Mala and me to stay. It will be better for Tasha as it's her first night. The C-section, overcoming the pain, a new baby, it's too much for Tasha to bear alone. You, my dear daughter, go home with the men. Come back in the morning and take over from us."

I sigh loudly, "How could you know from before what I was going say? It's frustrating at times."

Mom smiles back, "We mothers know our children and can read their minds."

"Ya...ya..." I mutter silently as she keeps reiterating the obvious, each time she gets an opportunity to do so.

As the nurse helps Tasha feed, mom takes me out too. As soon as we reach the men, she asks dad, "You all leave for home and take rest. Mala and I will stay with Natasha tonight. I have prepared dinner for you all. It just needs to be warmed."

She gives us a look that says, 'I am sure you all are capable of doing that at least?'

I let out a chuckle that is louder than I intend it to be. Shoot! Now all eyes are on me again. They all convey different emotions, but its mom's stare that I worry about the most. That look tells me that I am in deep shit!

"Well, Kaira, as you believe they are not going to be able to handle it, why don't you do the honours and serve dinner tonight? I am sure you are capable of doing that."

I kick myself mentally and scowl before replying when Sam lets out a loud laugh.

"Really mom? C'mon, I think dad and I will be able to handle it better. Kai is known to burn water. I don't think we want to destroy delicious food."

He jabs me humorously in my ribs. Even dad and Baig uncle are smiling. I don't even look at Drew, but I am sure he too is. I grunt and exclaim, "Shut up Sammy! That was years ago. I can cook a little now, or at least better than you."

"Kai, sweetheart, it was a general comment, not an attack at you. However, now you all should go. It's been an exhausting day, and you all must be hungry. Mala and I will ask for something from the kitchen here."

"Okay! Bye for now, Mom. I will be here by noon if it's kk?"

"Yes, once you come, we will leave. Tomorrow only one of us will stay back. Now go. Good night!"

As we all turn to leave, I remember our conversation and suddenly stop.

"Hey stop!"

Sam, who is walking behind me, bangs into me. Dad and uncle stop in their tracks and look at me questioningly. I hear Sam cursing me, "Kai, are you mad? What do you think you are doing?"

"Kaira, sweetie, you okay?"

This was from my dad who is hurriedly walking towards me. Shoot, I am so going to get a scolding… again! I curse myself and get ready to face the music for my impulsive behaviour.

"Oh, I am sorry… sorry! It's just that I suddenly remembered that we had not thought of a name for Angel."

They all go ballistic with their comments and stares.

"Really Kai!"

"God, you are crazy!"

"Kairaaaa…"

"Okay! It is a little silly, but it's just that the conversation was left incomplete, so…"

I shuffle my feet nervously while looking at the ground when mom speaks from behind, "Both names are lovely. If there are no more suggestions, then we can decide on one of them?"

I kiss mom softly on her cheek. As always, she saves me from further embarrassment.

We reach home and I set the table meticulously. Drew and uncle Baig join us for dinner. Since everyone is tired, we eat quietly and disperse.

Sam and I clear up the kitchen after everyone leaves for bed. The moment I reach my room, I feel all the emotions which I have bottled up since I heard of Drew flooding in. Seeing him again after four years brings back painful memories which I had repressed with great effort.

Our affair had caused nasty vibes between both the families. With time, we all had moved on and the relations got better. But that one mistake had left its cruel mark on all our souls.

10

Overnight, I turned into this calm and somewhat sorted adult who had lost the lustre for life. But the sombre and quiet me was causing more worry to all my loved ones. So, to everyone's relief, even though it took time, counselling helped restore some of my impulsive, child-like craziness again. Time heals all wounds, it sure helped me realize I did not have to be responsible like Tasha and Sam. I could be myself while being responsible for my deeds.

Living life zealously but with responsibility is the essence of who I am. Finding that balance between adulthood and childhood was tough, but I achieved it. It was a lesson that I learned the hard way.

I hug my pillow tighter as I walk down the memory lane after four long years.

I met Drew for the first time when he came home for his vacations. When Tasha and her family moved to Mumbai, Drew stayed back to finish his schooling. When uncle got posted, Drew had just finished his ninth grade and had insisted on staying back to finish schooling in Tehran only. Uncle had reluctantly agreed to avoid complications for Drew due to the education system. So, Drew was only a name when I met Tasha.

Drew is a year older than Sam. So, when he first came over for the holidays, it was like having another brother around. We loved irritating him, and in return, he would bully us. As the years passed, things changed. After his higher secondary, Drew went to London for further studies, and that was that, or so I thought. When Drew came home a year later, he was a changed person. The boy we knew was now a man. Experience and maturity shone out of him. I had heard London smartens you, but in Drew's case, I saw a living example. There was a new swag to his whole demeanour. He was confident, frank and very charming; a little too bold now. His British accent and well-endowed body were to die for. For a teenage girl like me, he was Salman Khan and Tom Cruise rolled into one!

I was happily surprised and totally tongue-tied. My heart was beating at a crazy pace. In fact, it beat so fast that I thought I was going into a cardiac arrest. I remember sweat break out on my forehead and couldn't understand what was happening. He kept speaking and for the first freaking time in my life, I couldn't get a single word out of my damn mouth.

People say hormones are high in teenage years, but mine were shooting through the roof. I was in love (or so I believed). I was nervous and coy whenever he was around. For the very first time in sixteen years, I was feeling emotions that were alien to me. I was conscious of my appearance all the time. Due to my braces and pimples, I avoided being around Drew. Gosh, he was so perfect! But I guess he hardly ever noticed me, though for me he had become my Mills and Boon hero…my Romeo…my everything.

Tasha, who had guessed my feelings, tried to dissuade me. She was uncomfortable with the changes in her brother. But he was her brother, my bestie's brother… how could he be wrong. So, I overlooked her warnings. Despite being against it all, she always supported me, especially when Drew teased me on the rare occasions that we were together in a room.

When Drew went back after his holidays, I cried for days as if I had lost something precious. I would mop around, snap at odd times, was rude to all. Something had changed in me. Now when I think about it, I feel every teenager goes through these bouts of emotional upheavals in the name of love.

I simmered down after a huge argument with Sam, about something very trivial. The fight shook me bad because even Tasha got upset with me after Sam stormed out. I have never seen Tasha this angry as she was that day. But it was the exact dose I needed to realize how difficult and stupid I was being with my silliness.

Her reprimand had a magical effect on me. I apologized to Sam and started giving importance to what mattered: my studies and my future. I had a dream to fulfill: my Café Library.

It was during the time I was working towards my goals that Sam acknowledged Tasha as an individual, and not just his sister's best friend. He was impressed knowing that meek Tasha had reprimanded me for my misbehaviour on his behalf.

Well, as time flew by, I continued to work hard and got an English Honors degree. Tasha, on the other hand, pursued Home Science. She is still happy managing the home. No one can work miracles with minimal resources like her. A lot of the décor suggestions for my Café came from her.

I yawn loudly and get startled by the sound coming from outside the room. OMG, it's been nearly thirty minutes since I have been sitting in the same place.

Wow! Jogging through the memory lane sure is an exhausting task! I get off the bed and move to the door. Surely everyone at home should be asleep by now. I tiptoe towards the kitchen to get a glass of water and check on the sound, just to be sure. Is Sam still drinking?

"Hey, Sammy, what are you doing up at this hour?"

I catch him by surprise as he sputters the drink all over the floor. Lol…!

"Shit Kai, what is wrong with you?"

"Hey, I thought you heard me. How could I know that you were in dreamland? Anyway, why are you still up? Dad sleeping?"

"Ya, and I could ask you the same. Why aren't you asleep? Is it the same reason…all of a sudden…after four years…hmmn…?"

I loved this about Sam. He never really beats around the bush. I hesitatingly reply in a soft tone, "Ummn…ya, I guess you are right. I think you should stop drinking and go now. You have work tomorrow. I am on holiday, so… nite nite Sammy!"

I slowly turn towards my room when Sam calls out worriedly, "Hey, Kaira, you doing okay na? Drew being here is not going to be a problem for you, right?"

I first think of brushing him aside, but I know I won't be able to pull it off, so I speak honestly, "I won't say it was easy meeting him again after so long. But I am much stronger now and I am long over the infatuation. I know what love means, having seen you with Tasha, or mom with dad, or for that matter, even Baig uncle and aunty. When I truly fall in love, it will be different, but it will be instant, deep and solid, I know that."

He sighs deeply. It is like he is holding on to each breath as I speak. And my answer relieves his tension.

"I'm glad you are fine. He is here for a while, so I wanted to be sure you're okay. Now I can sleep well. Thanks for letting me know... good night. And take care."

I whisper softly, "I love you, big brother."

"I love you too, baby sister. See you in the morning."

Time has changed us all. I may no longer be that star-struck girl. The crazy, totally impulsive and overconfident girl learnt where solid ground is and what is important in life. She now lives life with joy, gymming with her bestie, loving her cafe and her friends there. Time made sure I relook at where I want life to go and how.

11

When I return to my room, my eyes notice the frame with a picture of Tasha and me. It was the one we had clicked at our graduation ceremony. We both were dressed in ink blue gowns with shoestring sleeves. We looked our best and felt it too. It was the first time we were dressed this way. We felt like grown-ups for the first time in our lives. Seeing the picture makes me go back in time again.

I remember we were often the source of male attention. I enjoyed flirting but never got serious with anyone. My reasons were obvious, my infatuation with Drew had never ceased. In fact, it had increased with every visit. Each time it would feel like he took a small piece of me back with him. It seems melodramatic now, but at that time, he meant the world to me. On the other hand, Tasha was dating my brother. Sudden change in circumstances made us disclose their affair to mom sooner than planned.

I still remember they were sharing a romantic moment at the coffee shop near our college. They were amidst a hot kiss when I had crashed in on them. Tasha's phone was with me, and her dad had been calling, so I had to interrupt.

She turned pale as she tried to comprehend what he was saying. Sam and I panicked. We waited for the call to end. I put my arms around her as I saw tears falling. Sam hurriedly got a bottle of cold water for her.

"What happened? Is everything kk at home? What did uncle say?" Gosh! We had so many questions. She told us everything between tears and hiccups, leaving us astounded. I still remember my impulsive retort.

"What? Are you kidding me? We still have six months left to complete our graduation. How the hell can he even think of getting you married?"

I agitatedly started pacing across the tiny coffee shop. A regular occurrence with Sam is that the minute I turn ballistic, he eases out. I think my craziness always brings things in perspective for him, huh! Well, that day when he opened his mouth, he stunned both me and Tasha.

"Well, Kai, he can do anything he wishes to. After all, he is Tasha's father; he will always think of his daughter's well-being. I think the only solution to avoid this arrangement is by confiding in mom. I was going to do it after you girls graduated, but we don't have the time now. By the way, Tasha, when is your dad arranging this meeting?"

Still crying and hiccupping, Tasha spoke, "I think for this weekend, Sam… oh Sam…"

She continues sobbing uncontrollably.

Shit! This was frustrating. But seeing Sam in control, I felt sure things will be fine. We spoke to mom, who asked Mala aunty to convince uncle. God is great indeed!

Surprisingly, all were in agreement, but we were to wait till our graduation. Which was exactly what we wanted. And during this time, we knew Drew was planning to come home for a long break. After the holiday, he planned to settle in Dubai, a new job in a new country. I never knew that this break would change our lives forever.

Patience was never a trait I possessed, but for the first time, I kept calm. Tasha and I were officially graduating, and we had completed twenty-one years of living on earth. I started interning with my literature professor. I would build the foundation for my dream, my café library in future. So, with my internship, I pursued a business diploma program. Tasha was on cloud nine as both the parents had sanctioned her wedding.

She knew about my feelings towards Drew and my desire to pursue a serious relationship with him. She discouraged me at every step of the way, and I was my usual stubborn self.

When I think of it now, I feel she knew her brother's attitude towards life and didn't want her best friend to be involved in any mess with him.

The wedding preparations started. I knew the sudden change in my appearance had surprised Drew. He never really said anything, but I noticed him staring from the corner of his eyes. I made sure I was always around him, hoping for some response. I would converse with him about anything and everything. It was during one of these conversations that he finally asked me out and I immediately agreed.

The moment I was waiting for was finally here. In the confines of my mind, we were now a couple. Amidst the maddening wedding preparations, we managed to steal time for ourselves. I was completely besotted by him, or so I believed. His care and attention made me assume that he too was in love with me. There was a time when he had clasped my hand and didn't let go till we reached home. For me, it had been the most special moment till then. I looked at him, hoping he would say something, but he didn't. The trip ended quietly; he just waved goodbye and left.

Due to the wedding, his room had been taken over by gifts and guests. So he had rented an apartment some ten minutes away from home. Many times, we would sneak away to his place to spend time alone where we would listen to music, watch movies or just talk over a glass of wine.

It was here that he kissed me for the first time. I had never been kissed before, so the first time had been a little awkward. Though the soft touch of his lips had sent goose bumps all over my body. But something was amiss. I couldn't say what. The kiss had felt nothing like Tasha had described. I didn't really enjoy it the way I had hoped I would.

I did not think much of it, considering it was my first. Not everyone gets it right the first time. And from what I saw on Drew's face, I think he enjoyed it, so I kept quiet.

It did not occur to me that he hadn't bothered to check my comfort. He abruptly got up and poured himself a drink. Leaving me feeling confused and red-faced. Maybe it was me, after all Drew was experienced. He had boasted of his accomplishments with his past girlfriends. It had hurt to hear him talk about his adventures, but I couldn't expect him to be a virgin like me. He was, after all, twenty-five years old.

It was nearly two months since Drew and I were dating. The wedding was another month-and-a-half away. Drew was leaving a week after the wedding. The clock was ticking and I kept hoping he would pop the question or at least confess his feelings. We did kiss many times and each time I felt nothing but awkward and a tad disgusted. Like a fool, I did not give it much thought. My mind was telling me something that my heart refused to believe.

One day we were returning from a party, I was a bit tipsy… must have been that extra margarita Drew forced me to drink. I was in no state to go home. We decided to go to his apartment for coffee. Once I would get sober, he would drop me home – that was the plan.

In the elevator, Drew started kissing the nape of my neck. His touch got bolder and he pulled me closer in an intimate embrace.

I allowed him, not only because I was too high, but because I felt that this would help establish our relationship. I tried to enjoy myself.

I guess he was high on alcohol and maybe something more. I don't remember how we reached his apartment. Gosh, that evening comes back to me in disjointed flashbacks.

I recall finding myself on the sofa, semi-nude, with him on top, bare bodied. He was hungrily kissing my neck and squeezing my breasts with his rough hands. No! I wasn't enjoying it… I was feeling pain and disgust. I tried protesting, but he wasn't listening. I even outstretched my hands to push him away; he pinned me down and continued to devour me like a hungry wolf.

I really tried to enjoy, but his touch… his touch was making me feel sick by the minute. I allowed him to get more intimate thinking it would help, but the second I heard the noise of him unzipping his pants, I wanted to run away. He was trying to yank my panties down while freeing himself too. That was when I made use of all my strength to push him away. I remember him coming on me again, but I got up and moved to the opposite side of the sofa. He looked disturbed; I quickly found my bra and dress and put them on. That's when I had realized how far I had nearly gone.

I was about to say something to diffuse the situation when he spoke. His voice was slurring, and his gait was unsteady. I suddenly realized how drunk he was. His words killed whatever buzz that was left in me from the alcohol I had consumed. He growled loudly, "What the fuck, Kaira? Why are you being such a prude? This is what you have been begging for… so why are you behaving like a fucking virgin now? You kiss like a dead fish, at least you should be better experienced at sex."

I stood there shocked. Unsure if I had heard right. I stammer, "Drreeww... Drew! What on earth are… are you talking about? Wh… wh experience?"

He laughed like a hyena, and exclaimed, "Ohh come on, you have been hitting on me for years. You are no innocent with the way you move and flirt. Why do you think I took you out all this while? Why do you think I have been going around with you? If you had been some other woman, we would have had sex long back. It is just that you are Natasha's friend that I have been slow."

Hot tears burned my cheeks as they rolled down. I squeaked, "What are you saying?"

He gesticulated wildly and retorted, "Listen, I am not in the mood for a so-called romantic conversation. Are you staying for a good fuck? If not, then get out!"

I didn't realize that tears were running down my cheeks and ruining what little make-up I had on. I unknowingly fidgeted with my hair, making them look unruly. I stood there, a total mess, unable to understand what I had seen and heard. I couldn't believe it was Drew talking. I knew him; he wasn't like this… or was he?

He kept blabbering nonsense in his drunken stupor. I continued listening to him reduce my love for him to nothing but carnal desires. I was frozen in time with shock. I kept looking at him thinking it's a horrible prank. I even told myself that it's the alcohol talking, but no! This was something else…

He stopped talking. I waited for him to say something… just anything to stop my heart from breaking, but he just kept mum. Once he was dressed, I looked at him in the hope that he would drop me home, but he stormed out of the door, leaving me standing there. Leaving me stranded and lonely.

I don't remember how long I stood there, hoping for him to return. After what seemed like forever, I finally accepted that he was not coming back. I freshened up and went home. Thank god Mumbai is a safe city even at midnight for lone girls like me. I don't remember the journey at all. I just remember going straight to Tasha's house.

12

I stare at Tasha's door for the longest time, not knowing what to do. I think it was the watchman who rang the bell for me. He had followed me upstairs, doubting something was amiss. Luckily, Tasha answered the door instead of her parents or nosy guests. I must have looked as devastated as I felt, because she pulled me in and dragged me to her room. I could hear aunty and Tasha conversing indistinctly. But I was sooo zoned out that I couldn't understand anything. I knew Tasha was my safe haven, my bestie.

I started sobbing once again at my pitiable state. Unlike my usual strong self, capable of handling anything, I was having a breakdown. My self-respect, my self-worth, my confidence, everything was shattered.

I don't remember telling Tasha anything. But I must have spoken because she kept me by her side and didn't let me go home. I am guessing she spoke to Sam and convinced him to explain to everyone. I don't remember clearly.

Even today, as I stand by the window looking at the brightly shining moon, I cannot remember anything clearly about that night. I only know what Tasha told me later. She told aunty I was there for a sleepover. She told Sam that we were trying outfits for the wedding. My bestie, the honest and pure one, lied to the two people who mean the world to her. And she did all this for her stupid, immature and impulsive friend, who did not deserve it.

For a brief moment, I snapped back to life. Seeing her made me cry again, and I cried until there were no tears left. I held on to her as if she was my lifeline. She held me all night, not saying anything to me, just being there. I lay in her lap in a fetal position and slept like a baby.

In the early hours of the morning, I got up to find her still sitting by my side. She looked like she hadn't slept a wink. I just went into her arms and poured out what I remembered of the previous night's events. I told her how Drew left me all alone in the flat, how I took the rickshaw.

She was furious with her brother's irresponsible behaviour. But even then, I didn't let her blame him. I was still hoping that it was the alcohol. I wished secretly that the person I had been dating for nearly two months now wouldn't be this person. There was a small flicker of hope that it was a freaking nightmare and everything would be back to normal.

I remember begging Tasha to come with me to meet him and clear the night's misunderstandings.

"Please Tasha, you have to come with me. I need to see him. I mean, speak to him. I am sure he was under the influence of alcohol or some drug slipped to him at the party. He was not the same person I have been with all this time. He was someone else. Please, tell me you would take me to him once. I won't be able to rest until I speak to him."

"Okay, okay! I think you are making a big mistake, sweetheart. I have been warning you against him for a long time. I know him, and he is not at all what you imagine him to be. You think you are street-smart, but you are a baby compared to him. He is too shrewd and conniving for you to handle."

"No! Shut up! You are wrong, and I will prove it to you. How about we go see him before your wedding fittings? His house is on the way."

She caressed my forehead lovingly and replied," Okay... Now let's just sleep okay? I don't want our mothers questioning us later, sleep now Kai… good night."

I remember her slipping into the sheets beside me and falling asleep the moment her head hit the pillow. Poor thing! She must be exhausted. She had watched over me through the night. Now that I was awake, I was restless and desperate to see Drew.

I waited till 7.30 a.m. before getting out of bed. I met aunty on my way out who was surprised to see me awake this early.

"Good morning Kaira. Are you okay? I have never seen you up this early ever since you entered college life. Do you need anything?"

"Oh! Good morning aunty! No… I mean, yes… I'm good. I just wanted to get home to finish some work before Tasha and I left for the trials."

"How about some coffee before you leave?"

I was in no state to have coffee. I was worried about meeting Drew. I don't recall what I said, but I left asap, not realizing that my odd behaviour must have worried her. I didn't think she would call mom and tell her about it. Though I remember for sure Mom didn't say anything when I reached home. She let me go to my room without questions.

Even to this day, I wonder how I could have been so naive and stupid. How could I not have seen through his intentions? Why did I not trust my bestie who kept warning me? Why did I have to believe I was smart and worldly-wise? I was just a regular girl trying to go the extra mile to impress a man. Trying to fit into shoes that were never meant for her, nor were her style.

That day, I was taught a lesson for a lifetime: One can be, behave, act even pretend to be smart, but the world out there is shrewder, harsher and way more cruel than one's imagination.

There is no harm in being impulsive, over friendly or an extrovert, but always be cautious and responsible for your actions.

At sharp 11.30 a.m. that day, I knocked on Tasha's door again. As planned, we were first going to see Drew and then for the trial of her engagement outfit. I later realized that though mom had said nothing, she was keeping an eye on me. So, when aunty heard of our plans, she called mom.

We reached Drew's house by noon. He wasn't expecting us. We knocked, waiting for him to open the door. I was shivering out of sheer nervousness and fear. My mouth and throat were parched. After ten minutes of waiting, we used the spare key that was with Tasha.

When Tasha and I entered the house, we were startled by a strange smell that hit us. I slowly walked into the sitting area to see beer bottles and wine on the table. A hookah stood on the side table and its embers were still red. The room was in shambles, there were cigarette butts tossed around, the cushions were on the floor and dirty dishes piled up in the kitchen sink and on the floor. Tasha and I exchanged fearsome looks. "This was not the state of the room when I left last night. In fact, I vaguely remember putting the cushions and a few other things back in place as I waited for him to return."

Just then I saw a lady's shoes under the sofa and felt a churning in my stomach. I picked it up and turned to Tasha. She immediately tried to drag me out of the place. I was too dumb to gauge what was happening. But she had already understood everything. Despite all her efforts, I refused to leave and instead went further in to find Drew. As I slowly moved towards the door, I heard loud moans. I increased my pace, not caring whether Tasha was following me. I opened the door with shaking hands in a false hope… maybe it was a cat… maybe he was watching porn… maybe….

The sight in front of me broke my heart, my dreams, my strength. I had walked into a scene straight out of a B-grade film. Right there in front of me, Drew was fucking a girl, riding her like an untamed, wild horse. She was moaning and groaning with pleasure. Wasn't she the girl he had introduced as his friend's girlfriend? I shut my ears, but my eyes refused to close. He looked like a ruthless predator happily devouring his prey. The look on his face was filled with pure lust.

My sob made the two look at me. The girl looked embarrassed. The surprised look on his face would always stay with me. However, there was no remorse or guilt. In fact, I think I saw him smiling slyly as he went on with his business. At that moment it struck me like a lightning bolt – he just did not care. It had been me and my adolescent fantasies about him. I was the fool living in a fool's paradise. His agenda was clear from day one.

Tasha walked towards me, and without even looking at her brother, she pulled me out of the room. Seeing his sister briefly enter the room made him stop screwing the girl. Until then, he had been enjoying himself. He hurriedly covered himself and tossed a bed sheet on the naked girl.

We had just reached the door when Drew called out. Dressed in his boxers, sweating from top to toe, he breathed excitedly and smiled sarcastically, "What are you doing here, Kai baby? I thought I made myself clear last night. As you were not ready to jump into bed, I was no longer interested. If you changed your mind, you should have come alone instead of bringing my sister along with you."

Hearing such brashness from this lecherous bastard astonished me. I did not know what to say or how to react. When all of a sudden Tasha exclaimed, "Shut up Drew! Have a heart and at least show some respect for my presence in the room. I tried warning Kai about the ass that you are. She refused to see it… she could see just good in you. God knows how. Worse, this idiot thought you were in love with her."

By now the other girl had dressed up and quietly slipped out of the house. Drew laughed hysterically and retorted, "In love! Are you for real? Who spoke of love? She made herself available all the time. She literally threw herself at me. I never gave her reason to think I was interested in her. Her interest was obvious, so I pursued her lead. But love? Hahaha… You have got to be kidding! She is not even my type. I like them experienced, expressive and confident, not prudes like her."

Tears once again welled up in my eyes and I gasped out loud, making Tasha tighten her grip on my arm.

His words were like splinters piercing through my skin. I felt my heart would explode. God, I felt dirty and cheap. Where I was considering marriage and a happily ever after, he was just enjoying, like a stray dog enjoys a bone tossed towards it.

I stood there dripping in shock and hurt, cursing myself for this situation and my stupidity. Suddenly, out of nowhere, a hand slapped Drew hard across his face. It was his mother.

I don't know when Mala aunty had walked in. I think I saw someone move back near the entrance door, but I am not sure. I looked back at aunty. I don't know how much aunty had heard, but by the fury on her face, I think she had heard enough. I had frozen completely. So much so that when two pairs of familiar hands held me from either side, I didn't even realize my mom was holding me.

That day, I had felt a part of me dying. Nothing was going to be alright again. My beliefs, dreams and confidence lay at the feet of this stranger. A man I did not actually know.

13

I can still hear his words echoing in my ears, like a sharp, poisonous knife stabbed deep into my heart. What had supposedly been love for me had been fun and frolic for him, an easy lay. My emotions and feelings had meant nothing to him.

I have no recollection of how we reached home. I just vaguely remember Tasha taking me to my room while holding me tight. My state had the mothers worried and they knew they couldn't hide it from the men for very long. But at the same time, they did not want things to spiral beyond control. Uncle is strict and orthodox. Dad is cool and a softy, but if wronged, he has a temper no one would want to face. And as for Sam, he is totally temperamental; you could never be sure how he would react. So, the situation was very delicate with the wedding day approaching fast. The negative effect it could have on all the relations would be unavoidable.

As days went by and I refused to leave my room, everyone started to worry. Till now, mom had somehow managed to keep dad and Sam at bay.

The poison of Drew's words had spread deep and wide. I tried everything I could to rise above it all, but I was getting sucked in deeper.

After days of insomnia and staring into empty space, the effects started showing on my face. I developed dark circles and started looking ill. The need to sleep had me secretly searching mom's cabinet for her sleeping pills. I grabbed the bottle and swallowed a fistful with some water. I don't know when I fell asleep, or even how I reached my room. I just remember floating high in the air, free from every emotion and every hurt.

If Tasha had not come to see me that afternoon, I would not have been alive. When she saw me sleeping, she was going to leave. It was when she saw the half empty bottle of meds lying on the floor that she panicked and called mom. Fear and panic caused mom to call Sam immediately, letting the cat out of the bag. With the speed of lightning, Sam and dad were home with our family doctor in tow.

I was in no state to be taken to the hospital; it would mean filing a report, and cops would have to get involved. He flushed out the meds and put me on some antidote for a speedy recovery. My actions shook the foundation of my house. Everyone saw a side of dad that put fear of god in all. Even mom had kept quiet in face of such fury.

Tasha and Sam had their first serious fight. Seeing dad this angry had shaken her, but having Sam berate her too broke her down. Mom had called Mala aunty, who had already spoken to uncle about the situation. Now everyone knew, and everyone was in shock. Even Drew was stunned because this was something no one had expected from the supposedly invincible Kaira. When I finally woke up, the atmosphere reeked of stress and an impending disaster. I feebly opened my eyes and looked at everyone in the room. Except for Drew, everyone was there. I had no idea of the havoc I had created, nor that Sam had beaten Drew pretty bad. Seeing everyone so tensed, I, like an idiot said the first thing that came to mind, "Okay guys, who died?"

All hell broke loose!

"Are you mad?"

"Who takes pills without a prescription?"

"Why would you want to do something so stupid?"

"Don't we matter? How would we live without you in our lives? If not for Tasha, we could have lost you for good."

I could see the worry, fear and anger on every face. I realized how I had let one person pull me down, when there were so many to pull me up. It dawned upon me that nothing, and I mean *nothing* mattered more than these people in my life, *my family*. I slowly sat up on the bed to apologize profusely,

"I'm so sorry. I just desperately wanted to sleep, so did not see how many pills I can take. Please don't be so angry. I really am sorry. I promise to never be this stupid ever again for as long as I live."

But again, everyone shouted!

"Shut up sis…"

"You never think before opening that mouth of yours. Do you?"

"Kaaaiii…"

Ok, that was a stupid thing to say again, but at least everyone looked more animated. I had opened my eyes to sad, gloomy and upset faces, but now they all had some life to them. I know I had been careless and irresponsible, but the hurt and pain had been unbearable and will always be.

As I observed everyone in the room, I got the feeling of impending doom. Something was being hidden from me. There was anger, disappointment and hurt on faces around. And no one seemed to be looking at the other. I had really goofed up everything in my naivety.

I imploringly looked at mom for help, but just then, the doctor came in with his psychologist friend with him. She sat with me for forty-five minutes, talking and asking a million questions. It was then that I realized what a close call it had been.

14

I remember being confined to bed for the next few days. I could see things were not right. Tasha was never around like before. She would come when dad and Sam were at work and leave before they arrived. Dad checked on me, but never spoke more than a few words, which in itself was a statement that he was not over my reckless behaviour. Then there was Sam, who refused to take the bait when I troubled him. Usually, he would be on my case for the smallest thing I said, but now, nothing.

Mala aunty and uncle didn't visit again. Something was wrong... terribly wrong. I waited for the right opportunity to speak to Tasha, but she always avoided answering.

But the day I got out of bed, Tasha stopped coming over. I called incessantly; she neither picked my calls nor called me back.

In eleven years, Tasha and I had never been far from one another. So, her avoiding my calls and not berating me for my actions worried me. This silence was killing me, along with the creepy atmosphere at home. Being shut out was the worst punishment ever; I would rather face everyone's wrath. This was my fault and I could see everyone paying for it.

I was hoping jumping into the wedding preparation again once things settled would help. But Tasha's elusiveness and the silence at home worried me. Finally, I went to the one person who

I knew would answer my questions – mom. I pestered her till she was forced to open the Pandora's Box.

She was in the guest bedroom hanging the wedding clothes when I cornered her.

"Mom, what on earth is going on? Dad and Sam are angry with me; I understand. I messed up. But where is Tasha? Why aren't the wedding preparations going on? What is happening? I know I was stupid and goofed up big time, but even I wasn't expecting this outcome. It was not my intention to hurt and disappoint everyone."

She stopped her work and patiently replied, "Kai, I agree this is a mess created by you and Drew. But it's a mess that has affected both families. Your mistake has left a serious impact on your dad and brother's minds. They can't get over the fact that you could take such a step. They know nothing about what happened that night, but seeing you at death's door has put the fear of god in them. Even I cannot get over Tasha's scream that day. So, what should I tell them?"

I looked at her with angst in my eyes, "I know mom! It is an unforgivable mistake, a big one. But mom, it was exactly that, a mistake. It was not intentional or planned. So why are Sam, Tasha, dad and the rest of the family suffering? Why hasn't Tasha come to visit me in the last four days? She is not even picking my calls, nothing."

Mom sighed sadly. I could feel her measuring her words as she spoke. Maybe she was afraid I would behave recklessly again. "Sweetheart, everything has been bought to a halt. The wedding has been postponed indefinitely for now. I am not even sure if it will take place. Dad and Mr Baig are not speaking to each other. Mr Baig threw Drew out of his house and has cut off with him. Sam nearly killed Drew when he came to apologize and check on you. So, everything is in a mess. Mala and I are not sure how to handle it for now. We both are quiet. Waiting, watching and praying."

My heart sank. This was so unfair. People I love were being punished because of my stupidity.

"What about Tasha?"

"Well, that poor girl is paying the price for no mistake of hers. Sam was way too angry with her for not telling him about your crush. She even got fired by her father for no fault of hers. Now she is banned from coming here or talking to you."

I gasped loudly and exclaimed, "But that's so not fair. I am the one in the wrong, so why is she paying the price for it? And how could Sam be angry with her? When they were going out, I didn't tell you, so why would she? BFFs don't snitch, mom. He should know that, shouldn't he?"

I looked at mom with tears brimming in my eyes. I was so ashamed of what I had dragged the family into because of my carelessness. But one thing I did know, I had to correct this.

"Mom, what do you suggest I should do in order to make this right? It is my mistake, and I am the only one who has to correct it."

She sighed and continued with her work, avoiding eye contact, "Mala and I have not yet announced that the wedding is off. We have kept it quiet. As I said, we are waiting for some more time to pass before we try to speak to the men once again. There are still a few weeks left; till then we will continue preparing in a hope that all goes well."

I looked at her in sheer disbelief. "Mom, we cannot leave things like this. There are only a few weeks left with a lot to do. So, I have a suggestion, if you agree."

She sighed wearily, but I knew she would help me make things right.

"How about we invite the Baig family for dinner, without Drew? We call dad and Sam home early on some pretext. After that, I speak to everyone, apologize for my behaviour and ask for forgiveness. Then request them to not ruin two lives for a mistake I made."

"Wow Kai, do you really think you will be able to pull it off? I know you are my competent daughter, but this is a tough situation. And knowing your dad, he could create a fit!"

"Ya, I know! But it's at least better to have it all out in the open. Right now, everyone is living with depression and the wedding hangs in suspense. As for dad creating a fit, well, I am his daughter, so chillax! Please, you just call Mala aunty and tell her to get everyone. The rest I will manage."

"Kai, Drew is no longer in Mumbai. His father shipped him off to another country immediately after the incident."

"Ohh..."

At this moment, Sam and Tasha mattered more than Drew leaving India. My pain was like a thorn embedded deep within and the pain was mine to bear. My family didn't deserve to bear the brunt of it.

That evening, while I waited for everyone, I swung between nervousness and fear. I knew that I could make everything right. I was, after all, the fulcrum of my family. Mom's words struck me; this sure was a huge responsibility, and I just had to succeed at it.

I wiped my sweaty hands before opening the door when the bell rang. Dad was reading a novel, while Sam watched the TV in the lounge. I welcomed uncle and aunty and hugged Tasha, whispering into her ears softly, "You and I will talk later, so better be prepared for war. Let me handle this first."

Before she could question me or even reply to my threat, I called out to dad and Sam. They were shocked to see the Baig family there. Dad looked at mom angrily, and she pointed to me. I smiled sweetly, requesting everyone to sit.

I stood before them all with folded hands, contemplating my next words. I started twisting my hands, feeling sweat pour down my back as nervousness made me twitch. I think I was on the verge of a panic attack when I heard a reassuring voice,

"It's okay Kai, say what you have to…" It was my darling saviour, my mom.

With a deep breath, I began to speak.

"This is my entire family. We have all known each other for a long time. In fact, Tasha and I brought this family together. Each of you adopted us as your own and loved us unconditionally and equally."

I cleared my throat as emotions choked me. Everyone was just looking at me, waiting for my next string of words.

"Sam falling for Tasha was the best thing for us all. I know dad was super happy at the news."

I looked at dad to see him shake his head in affirmation. When I look at Baig uncle, he too was agreeing to this. I hugged myself before continuing to the tricky part.

"Well, I see both dads are in agreement here. So, I am sure you both will also agree that the recent spate of events was my fault, and not Tasha's. I know I should not have behaved the way I did; it was the biggest mistake of my life. But uncle, dad, I am solely responsible for my actions."

I went to dad and sat by his feet, held his hand tight and looked at him in the eyes as I said, "Dad, I am so sorry. I know I made a huge mistake, I was totally irresponsible. I am really ashamed of myself and my actions, I know I deserve to be punished. But dad and uncle, you both have disappointed me too. I am the only one at fault in the mess I created, so why are you all paying for it? Why is Tasha paying for it? You being angry with Drew is understandable; he hurt your daughter. But then you and Sam have hurt uncle Baig's daughter as well. So, he has the right to be angry too. All this… because of me…."

My voice cracks with emotions, while mom, Mala aunty and Tasha let out a few sniffles. Sam was sitting up, scowling while uncle Baig was giving a slight smile. Dad, on the other hand, started looking out of the window.

I gave everyone time to process my words while I too took a breather. I knew this was going to be difficult, but I wasn't aware that it would be so emotionally exhausting. I saw Tasha standing still in the corner, too surprised and worried to speak.

After a few seconds, I continued again, this time a bit more confidently, "What happened with Drew and me was unfortunate, but totally separate from Sam and Tasha's relationship. Being involved with Drew was my mistake, for which no one else should be punished. It is my lesson in life, one I will learn from so that I never repeat it again. But please tell me why Tasha should pay for my mistake? I know you haven't totally forgiven me, dad, but I am really sorry. I request you to not cancel the wedding because of me."

I folded my hands as I looked at all the adults apologetically.

I then turned to Sam.

"As for you Sam, I won't apologize to you because I don't appreciate you abandoning Tasha for no mistake of hers. I mean, how could you leave her or even think of it after everything she has done for you? In a way, your behaviour was worse than Drew's! I know you love me Sammy, but you made some commitments to Tasha too. How could you even think of backing away? And why? She is the same girl you stood up for in front of the parents, right? Now, at the first major crisis, you just left her! That, dear brother, is not what love is. So, dear family, please rethink very carefully before making any decisions because it affects everyone's life here. Again, I am really… really… sorry."

After saying this, I slowly walked out of the room, closing the door behind me. I hoped love would fill these cracks soon.

15

I splashed cold water on my face. Gosh! That was the toughest speech I have ever given. There was a knock at the door, but I already knew who it could be. I smiled and welcomed her, "Come in Tasha. Since when do you need to knock?"

"Since my friend and soul sister has grown so big that I am feeling small in front of her. I would never have guessed you could be so humble."

"Please, don't BS with me. I am too upset with you to pay heed to your kind words."

I looked at her with anger as I spoke, "Tasha, how could you not fight for what is right? I thought I had taught you better! The messy affair between Drew and me shouldn't have stopped you from standing up to Sam when he was wrong. How could you keep quiet? But what hurt me most was you not taking my calls. How could you? It is something I will never forgive you for."

I choked while speaking and hugged her tightly. Tears were running down our cheeks. The room was filled with love.

All of a sudden, Tasha started wailing loudly, "How could you do this, Kai? What if I had not come into the room? What if the doctor had not come on time? What then? If something had happened to you, I too would have died."

"Oh god Tasha! You are not getting rid of me so easily. But there is one thing that I have realized from all this. It is not just you who needs me, I need you more. You keep me grounded, and sane. Your silence compliments my effervescence. It is not just you or me, it is us, now and forever. But the next time you don't take my calls, I will kill you myself."

We both chuckled at my last statement and hugged each other tightly. We then lay on the bed, facing the ceiling while she updated me on what had been happening in this past week.

Shit! Can you imagine? A whole week had passed since that day! Well, the moms had kept quiet about it, but my stupidity unveiled the harsh facts. The fathers and Sam still didn't know the whole truth except that I had gotten drunk. Thank god for small mercies! But it was a close touch down. It seemed Sam whacked Drew pretty hard. Even though I knew that uncle had sent Drew away, but it was still a shock to hear Tasha confirm it.

Drew had been sent to Dubai immediately after that day, and even though the wedding was going to go as planned, Drew was not allowed to attend. Everyone agreed it would be an insult for my family, including me. I believed it was a little harsh because I was equally at fault. But a selfish part inside me relaxed, as I knew I wasn't ready to face him, not any time soon.

Everything continued as per schedule and the earlier plans. On the surface, nothing had changed; but still, a lot had.

I took the doctor's advice and kept my appointments with the psychologist. The counselling therapy helped me restore my confidence, but I became more cautious of the opposite sex. No man was ever going to call me easy or available again. The counsellor helped get my perspective in order and turn towards fulfilling my dreams. She encouraged my idea for the Café Library. But with the hustle bustle of the wedding, I put that dream on hold for a little longer. It was on my agenda the minute Tasha and Sam left for their honeymoon.

A shooting pain in my leg gets me back to reality. My leg has gone to sleep while I reminisce the past, but it was important too. Shoot, it is nearly 3 a.m. and tomorrow is going to be another busy day, especially at the hospital. Then I also need time to decorate Angel's room, so the rest of the story, later. Nite nite!

16

Morning comes way too soon for me. It is filled with chaos, just like every other Indian home. The men in my house are absolutely useless without their wives. I can hear dad and Sam going crazy for breakfast and for coffee. Like, this is a madhouse without mom and Tasha. As for me, I am so sorry, but this is so not my choice of job. I hate cooking and keeping house. I love my books, my Café and my daily interactions with people.

After Sam's wedding, we had gotten lucky. Our neighbours were selling their house and were kind enough to put an offer to dad. Which was a superb coincidence because we were also planning for a bigger home. Dad didn't think twice and accepted the offer. Everyone knows the crazy real estate prices in Mumbai. So even though the buying price was a little more with the extra premium charged by the 'kind' neighbour, it was too perfect to let go, so dad accepted. It took time, but everything worked out marvellously!

Slowly, we expanded the house, restructuring the whole floor into one. That way, we are all together, without affecting each other's privacy and life. Well, I am blessed to live in such a huge apartment in a city that is exploding due to lack of space.

When I leave my room, I am surprised to see dad cooking in the kitchen. Wow, now that is a first for sure, as for brother dear, he was packing tiffins for everyone. Wow, wonders never cease! I pull out a chair and then my phone to start video recording. Dad laughs while he hears me speak, "Now, this is live recording for mom and Tasha. The men of the house in the kitchen, like OMG! Mom, you sure need to see the state of your kitchen!"

I pan the camera around the entire kitchen and then shift focus on Sam. He exclaims humorously, "It sure is better than last night, mom. All she did was serve the food you had already prepared. She did not even clear the mess afterwards, which was worse than this, huh."

I turn the camera to selfie mode and say, "Such hoax, I cleared everything before turning in so Sam is BSing. Btw, what is that you are cooking? By the look of that, it was an egg, now it is a black burnt block, huh."

I pan the camera towards dad, just in time to see what he is doing, and it is disastrous. I hurriedly shut the camera and scream loudly,

"Dad, *dad!* What are you doing??? The milk has long overflown and spread on the stove. It is burning now. Uggh! The smell! Dad! Okay, that's it, guys! Out… *out* right now! You both go and sit. I will have everything on the table in fifteen minutes. Just give me space… go!"

I march them out of the kitchen when Sam quips, "Hey sis, need help?

"Hahaha!!! Thanks, but no thanks!"

The minute they leave, I see the disastrous state of the kitchen and feel like pulling my hair.

I quickly get sunny-side up eggs and toasted bread ready for breakfast. On the side, I quickly get the tea ready. Once everything is ready to serve, I set the table and let them eat while I get coffee for myself.

Did I mention that I am an absolute mess without my first fix of coffee? I am too slow, practically a zombie. So the adrenaline rush of this morning is a surprise for me too.

I sit with Sam and dad while enjoying my coffee and planning our visit to the hospital. Sam is in a hurry to see his wifey and Angel. Dad plans to visit in the evening after work. As for me, I would straighten up the house and take over the afternoon shift. Thus, relieving both moms to recoup. With all set, we take each other's leave. No one mentions Drew's presence, and I do not consider it important enough, so stalemate!

By the time I finally have the house to myself, the part-time maids have walked in. So, with them taking over the cleaning of the house, I get dressed. Despite taking an off, I sit down to tally the accounts of the previous day.

Business is good; goal accomplishment always brings a feeling of satisfaction. I finish reading the reports and cataloguing of the latest books. I take a quick glance through the most recent ventures and market updates. While I am wrapping up work, my mind wanders to the stranger I met at the Café yesterday. Wow, has it been just a day? It feels like a lifetime has passed. This unknown man has been tugging a corner of my heart that was closed for the past four years. I breathe deeply and when I open my eyes, I find him standing in front of me! I jerk up, rubbing my eyes only to realize I am daydreaming, again. Wow, who was he? I wish I knew.

Anyway, with my days' work done, I get ready to leave. I quickly check all the rooms and kitchen to make sure everything is in order. The house needs to be as per the standards set by mom. I quickly lock the house and make my way down. It is nearly

11.45 a.m.; I have another forty-five minutes to reach the hospital. I know I had said noon, but then no one better than mom knows how impossible that is with me. Time and me in sync? Ahhh… Never happens!

As I reach my bike, I hear someone calling my name. I turn to see Drew sauntering towards me. What is he doing here? Humph… why do I care? I continue to wear my helmet and prepare to leave when he reaches my side. He gives me a beaming smile; I return a wry one.

"Hi Kai…"

"Hey..."

"Are you going to the hospital?"

"Yeah, in fact, I'm late."

"Would you mind giving me a lift? My car is at the repair station, and I also wanted to go to the hospital."

"You want me to take you to the hospital on my bike… hmm?"

"Yes, if it is okay with you?"

"Drew, I don't want to sound condescending or rude, but I think a taxi will be a better option for you. My bike will not suit your stature and personality. So, I will see you later. Bye!"

I start my bike and ride away, not waiting for his answer. I look into the rear-view mirror and see him standing there forlorn, staring at me. The most amazing part of this encounter is that I do not feel anything, neither the previous hurt nor the tingling sensation I used to get whenever he was around me. I feel the cool breeze playing with my hair. Wow, to be emotionally free is a wonderful thing!

17

I ride with a happy mind and a liberated heart. The emotional freedom relaxes me while adding wings to my ride. Just a few minutes away from the hospital, disaster strikes. Shoot, I am feeling way too good, and now, this!

Okay, I know I was over speeding a bit, but my bike got more hurt than his freaking car! Ya ya yaa, you guess right, I have met with a small accident. Hey, please don't judge me! I know I am prone to accidents. But this time I got careless due to internal bliss and happiness. Shoot, nooo, it is big shit!! I just crashed my bike into Mr Mystery Man's car! Seeing him get out of the car gives me a feeling of deja vu.

It seems like I conjured him from thin air. I have had glimpses of this man bothering me at the oddest times. Like just this morning when he flashed right before my eyes unexpectedly, and now this. I am not sure what this means, but it is surely not what I need now. So here we are, unfortunately, not the perfect scenario again.

"OMG! It's you again! I guess we are destined to meet like this only. Btw, are you stalking me?"

He looks at me as if I have lost my mind. Maybe I have, huh. He sure roughs up another side to me.

"Ms Fireball, this wouldn't be my choice of place if that was my intention. I would have chosen better surroundings, not the middle of a random road. As for stalking you, hahaha, you sure think a lot about yourself!"

"Hey! You are mean. I was kidding, kk? You know, trying to diffuse a situation..."

He gives me a look I don't understand, but it sure makes me blush. I feel my heartbeat increase. It is an odd reaction to a complete stranger. I switch to my bike, getting ready to leave, when he speaks, "Hey Fireball, were you trying to diffuse the situation or escape it? Because I see no need for diffusion here."

Again Fireball? What the heck! Here I am trying to get away from these weird emotions, and this handsome stranger is challenging me! The one thing I never back down from is a challenge. And quite honestly, I had forgotten about the accident. So, I am forced to turn towards him again.

"Hey! What's with this name tag 'Fireball'. And hello! I have no reason to escape from anything. The shock of the accident freaked me out a bit, so I spoke instinctively."

I look up and see a smirk on his face. This man is having fun at my expense. How audacious! I am about to retort, when he speaks, "Well, in that case, you owe me for my damaged head. As for Fireball, I don't know why or where it came from, but it suits you. Don't you think?"

I grunt loudly and reply, "What on earth are you blabbering about? You and your head seem to be perfectly fine to me. It is your driving we need to discuss here. You did stop all of a sudden, with no warning!"

"Actually, it was the headlight of my car I was talking about. But now that you mention driving, from what I noticed, you were speeding and even jumped the previous signal. In fact, it looked like you were heading straight for my car."

"Whaaat???

"Fireball, are you sure you banged into my car by mistake and not intentionally?"

Shoot, this man is over smart and over the top! He seems to be enjoying my discomfort now. Finally, I meet someone who can get the better of me, or at least can try. And yes, he is handsome too.

"Okay, Mr Smarty Pants, you got me! It was your car and not you that I was headed for. I hate Mercedes cars, so seeing yours fired up my hatred. I just lost control and went straight for it."

How I kept my face straight, I don't know. How I did not burst out laughing at his expressions will remain a mystery. The look on his face was priceless. I have never seen anyone this stupefied before. When he continues staring at me with those stupefied brown eyes, I couldn't stop my loud, throaty laughter. It had been a while since I have laughed so loud and so freely. It felt amazing! He too starts smiling and then lets out a hearty laugh when he realises the joke was on him. Hmm… he has a great SOH (sense of humour, before you all wonder) and he has a great laugh too.

"I am sooo sorry, I just could not resist. You were trying to make me feel guilty, so I just had to outsmart you somehow."

"You sure did that, Fireball. I believed you too. It's rare for me to believe someone so easily."

"It was a pleasure sparring with you Mr… see you around."

Saying this, I turn away. I am just about to sit on my bike when another car passes by, inches away from me. The suddenness causes me to lose my balance. At one point in those milliseconds, I was sure I was going to say hello to death and not mother earth this time.

Once again, I am saved by those firm, and now, for some reason familiar hands. He yanks me towards him firmly; I can feel his heart pounding. I close my eyes tightly and hold on to his arms, pressing myself closer to his warm body. It takes me a while to get my nerves settled back and slowly pry my eyes open.

When I open my eyes, I find myself looking into the most amazing, warm, chocolate brown eyes. They remind me of my favourite hot chocolate fudge with caramel sauce. The intensity in those eyes makes me shiver with more than just fear. They are looking at me tenderly, making every nerve tingle and every hair on my body stand. He tightens his grip on me when he feels the shiver run through me again. I have never felt so safe and nervous at the same time. In fact, it takes a minute to realize he too is trembling… but why!

I slowly slide my hands up to his able shoulders for support. Our bodies are practically joined at the chest. My heart is thumping so hard that I am sure he can hear it. I can see emotions changing like the rainbow in his eyes, fear to concern to desire. I think he moves his head towards mine, or is it me! I don't know but the need to kiss is strong. Are we going to? Would we have kissed? I don't know. I was spellbound by the intense look in his eyes. What would have happened will remain a mystery because the loud honk from another car shakes us out of our dream-like state. I think we both are breathing really hard… or am I imagining it all? I attribute my dazed state to the adrenaline rush and to my near-death experience.

Pulling my hands away from his shoulders, I quickly sit on my bike. When I look up to thank my Mystery Man, I notice we have attracted a crowd. The traffic is held up and everyone was staring at us.

"Aye Romeo, romance ghar pe kar, sadak pe nahi"

"Abbey ghar pe jagah nahi hogi, issiliye!"

"Aye Romeo, aye!"

Mumbai is like this, never lewd, just crass... god!

A whistle from one of the boys shakes Mystery Man and brings him back to reality. He straightens himself abruptly, pulling his hands back, which are reaching out for me again. Instead, he adjusts his shirt and moves towards his car. I start my bike, saying a quite thank you without making eye contact and ride off quickly.

18

The wind cools the heat of my face, helping me calm down. It seems like eternity since I reacted to a man emotionally. I almost see myself as asexual, avoiding men and anything romantic. Today, these feelings jump out of nowhere and now I'm running for life.

By the time I reach the hospital, I am more in control. When I enter Tasha's room, I find Drew already there. He gives me a strange look, but who cares! I ignore him and look for mom, then at my watch. I am twenty minutes late, shit!

"Where are mom and aunty?"

I look at Tasha, but it is Drew who answers, forcing me to look at him.

"They left twenty minutes back. When I reached, I asked them to go. I assured them you were reaching in some time."

"Oh, thanks!" I turn to Tasha and smile, "Well, hello mommy dear, how are you doing? And what's this? Where are you hiding my niece?"

Tasha smiles weakly, and replies, "Oh, they have just taken her for a nappy change. I am doing good… doctor says I need to start walking within twenty-four hours of delivery. But Kai, the pain is unbearable at times. There is pain around the stitches, but the meds are taking care of it. Huh! I sure am in a better state than you!"

"What do you mean? I am absolutely fine! What seems to be wrong with me?"

I don't realize that I sound jittery. Nor do I realize that the incident with Mystery Man has affected me more than I could fathom. When I hear Tasha appease me, I try to calm myself. Gosh! What on earth is going on with me?

Tasha chuckles, "Hey Kai, relax! You look fine! It's just that there is mud on your cheek and a slight tear on your shirt near the shoulder. That is why I asked. Nothing to get so antsy about."

I fish out a wet tissue from my tote bag and wipe off the mud. Then I look for the tear. When did my shirt tear? When I left this morning, my shirt was alright, so when? Then I remember the accident with the Mercedes, and Mystery Man, shoot.

With that I remember how amazing being in his arms had felt and the swoon-worthy look he had. A gush of emotions totally different from any I had ever felt before hits me again. I am so lost in thoughts that I don't hear Tasha calling. Until a rough shake brings me back to my surroundings.

"Ouch, what?"

I wince at the touch and turn. It's Drew. I move away from Drew and go to Tasha, who looks at me with concern.

"What is wrong, Kai? You seem lost, everything is fine… right? What happened to you?"

"It's nothing to worry about. I just had a small accident OMW here, nothing major. The shirt must have torn then."

"If it was nothing, then why are you so flustered and lost? Something must have happened to have shaken you this badly."

Gosh, this is what happens when your bestie knows you so well. Just thinking of the accident brings him to mind, a man whose name I still didn't know. But right now, I had to appease Tasha, who was on my case.

"You better tell me what happened! We all have been telling you to sell that thing and get a car. You are rash and careless on that monster. I am guessing something big happened to make you look like this."

I look at her, lying in bed, weak from the operation, struggling with the newness of motherhood. It's not the time to burden her with silly details of my life. I smile at her and say, "Okay now, don't you even dare think of selling my second bestie. You know I have had my bike for like forever. Today, I just got unlucky, and it was a small accident, and this tear is from a fall, not the accident."

She gasps loudly, "What fall? Are you hurt? Should we call the doctor? Kaiii…."

Shit, me and my big mouth!! It's high time to push Mystery Man out of my mind; I am losing focus. I am not filtering information before speaking and now Tasha is waiting for me to speak.

I gather myself and reassure her,

"No Tasha, I am fine. You are the one who had surgery and needs to rest and not stress. Please relax, okay?"

She finally realizes I won't say anything, especially with Drew there. I change the topic, hoping to pacify her.

"Were Angel and you fine last night? Especially with the pain and discomfort."

"Well, it was amazingly easy only because both moms were here. They took turns all night with her changing, burping and crying. As for me, after the initial hiccups with feeding, I managed fine, I guess. In fact, they should be getting Angel back soon."

We get so involved in talking that we completely forget about Drew. He coughs lightly to grab our attention.

Both Tasha and I don't know what to say. He immediately quips, "I was wondering if any of you wants coffee…?"

With him around, avoiding conversations is not possible. I decided last night that I will acknowledge him as Tasha's brother and keep it cordial.

"Yes Drew, that would be amazing! The coffee I made tasted crappy. Please get only one as your sister is not allowed coffee. Not good for feeding mothers..."

Tasha says, "Hmm, all of a sudden, you seem to know a lot about feeding mothers. One coffee won't kill me."

"Hey, doctor's orders sweetie! As for knowing a lot, well, I did pay attention during those classes you forced me to attend with you. Remember those books you read out to me? Some of the information did register. So yaaa, I do know a little about feeding mothers..."

"God, you sound like a two-year-old who was forced to eat all the veggies."

"Shut up, bitch!"

We end our little squabble with a smile, once again forgetting about Drew.

Now, this is a thing with Tasha and me – when we are together, we don't need anyone else around. Even Sam tends to get envious about it.

Drew exclaims, "Umm… I think I should just go and get the coffee." That's when we remember his presence.

As soon as Drew leaves the room, Tasha asks to be propped up. She makes herself comfortable before restarting her interrogation. I just knew it was coming! I sometimes feel I am a mood enhancer for her. Like I am a relaxant for her husband.

"Okay, first let's clear the question that is on everyone's mind. Are you okay with Drew being here? I mean, not just in the hospital, but around the home and family."

I hurriedly shush her, "Babe you are still healing from surgery. You need to take care of yourself and the baby. Please don't worry about petty issues."

She gasps in disbelief.

"Petty issues? Like, really Kai?? We nearly lost you... remember?"

My voice turns soft as I slowly spell out, "Tasha, that was a long time ago. I don't say I have forgiven or forgotten, but I was equally at fault. I have no grudges against him anymore. Trust me, seeing him again was a good thing. At least now I know that I am over my infatuation. Besides, I think only he paid the price for something that we were both to blame. His return is good, especially for Mala aunty. I know she missed him a lot. So, where Drew's issue is concerned, you can chillax... okay?"

Tasha looks at me as if I have grown a second head! I laugh loudly only to find her eyes are nearly bulging out of her head.

"Gosh Tasha! That look on your face is frame-worthy!"

And before she realizes, I fish out my phone and I take a picture. This snaps her out of her shock. She protests loudly, "Hey, delete that picture. I look horrendous!"

"No sweetie, you look amazing! It's quite a Kodak moment, see?"

She looks at the picture and grunts in false disdain.

"I look like a maniac! But keep it, it's worth every bit. At least, I got to hear your signature laugh... I have been missing it for the past four years."

She places her hand on mine and says, "Remember Kai, you had a totally carefree laugh? It used to spread positivity and happiness to everyone around. It has been a long wait. So, anything is worth it to hear it again and again."

Tears run down my cheeks as she expresses her thoughts. I realize it's been long since I allowed myself to flow like this. Today

I feel liberated from all bondages and shackles. When I begin searching reasons, once again, out of nowhere, Mystery Man pops back into my head. Gosh! When and why did I start calling him Mystery Man? Why does my mind keep racing back to him?

Tasha jabs me with her index finger, "Okay Kai, now I *really* need to know what new has happened lately. Please don't say Angel is the cause for your comeback! That excuse would be a crappy one. Something has changed Kai… something good has happened to you… so start talking!"

I feign irritation and exclaim, "Uff! Miss Bond, don't over work your little mind. You know I will never hide anything from you. So, it's obvious I will tell you everything. But right now, you need to rest. Btw, don't you think Angel should have been here by now?"

I guess the nurse was standing out listening to our conversation. Lol! She promptly enters with Angel who is cooing happily I quickly sanitize my hands and move towards Angel.

"Saari Enty! Pahile baby ko mummy ka feed chahiye, phir aap baby ley sakte hai." She gives me a matronly look through her rimmed spectacles while signaling me to stand off.

She hands over Angel to Tasha who had propped her pillows and is ready to feed her. I watch this sight with absolute amazement. To see Tasha's maternal side was beautiful. She is always the homely one and being a mother came so naturally to her. We had read about feeding problems with new mothers, but Tasha feeds so naturally as if she has been doing it forever. She gently caresses Angel's tiny head while looking at her lovingly. The beautiful, eternal bond of emotions between the mother and child gives me goose bumps. I whisper a prayer for the safety of the family. As soon as the nurse leaves, Tasha is on my case again.

"Out with it, fast, before someone else interrupts."

Her switch from mom to friend was almost magical!

Before I could react, there is a knock on the door. It is Drew; he stands at the door with a cup of my favourite brand of coffee.

"Hey, where did you find Starbucks here? This hospital doesn't have one."

"No, there is one across the street. I thought, since I was getting coffee anyway, why not a decent one? I did not want to experiment with the coffee they serve here. This one is exactly the way you like it – Latte with cream and two spoons of sugar."

"Oh, I'll take that; however, I now prefer Mocha with no cream and one spoon of sugar. No issues, thanks a lot anyway. You can't come in right now as Tasha is feeding and I have no idea how long that takes."

"That's fine, I was anyway leaving. Dad called me for some work."

"Bye!"

He calls out just before I shut the door. I open it slightly with a questioning look in my eyes. "Kai, I wanted to thank you. I know if not for you, my parents would not have allowed me here. I know it's coming late, but I am sorry. I behaved like a bastard and was way out of line…"

He was in a mood to continue, but I do not plan on listening further. "Listen, Drew, it's kk. You don't have to apologize for anything. I was also stupid and equally wrong. As for you being here, I have no hand in it. It's the elders, and I agree with them. This is your family, and you need to be here with them. So, all is good. Bye."

I close the door quickly. Today is not the day to dig up the past. It's a day to celebrate freedom from those painful memories. I do not want anything to tie me down again; I am loving this feeling of freedom.

I amble towards Tasha who exclaims, "That was impressive and mature."

I shrug as if to say, 'Whatever!'

"Have you finished feeding her?"

"Yes, for now. Tell you what, why don't you burp her?"

"Hey, I don't know how."

She helps me prop Angel to my shoulder, while carefully holding her head. She asks me to pat her lightly till she burps.

I nervously carry her around and pat her lightly. All of a sudden, a loud noise is heard,

"BURP!!"

"Wow, what a *loud* sound for such a tiny one!"

We both laugh at Angel's cuteness. She falls asleep on my shoulder and I feel like the luckiest aunt in the whole world.

I excitedly narrate the sequence of incidents with Mystery Man from the day before at the Cafe to the one this morning. The near fall at the Cafe and the sparring that followed. Then our second crash this morning on my way to the hospital. She listens eagerly as I smile nervously, describing my brush with death and his quick reflexes at saving me again. I feel like Sleeping Beauty bought to life by the handsome prince riding in his white Mercedes instead of horse. Fear that she would laugh at the analogy makes me keep quiet, though it is an effort. But there is something I can't stop myself from telling her.

"Tasha, something surprising happened this morning which cemented the fact I was over Drew and that past... My signature laugh as you call it, was not my first today. I relished it before, during a special moment with Mystery Man."

"Hey, what are you saying? This I want to hear about."

I tell her about the prank I pulled in retaliation to his smartness, while we were arguing. Remembering his zapped look brings a smile to my face again, surprising Tasha. I finally tell her how I felt I had met someone with the same wavelength as mine.

"Wow, I go out of action for just one day, and you manage to find so much action in yours! But I am super glad. I have been waiting for my Kai to be back. Hearing that you pulled a prank like before and hearing your laugh makes me believe that she is back."

I sigh loudly,

"Good lord Tasha! Stop being so melodramatic, please! I agree it has been a while and yes, it felt good. I can't describe it but something broke loose, freeing me. Whatever it is, I am glad it happened. Now, enough! You please rest or everyone will take my case for keeping you up. We can talk more about it when you are better and back in action. Rest, sweetie."

Tasha sleeps happily while I turn to the window, smiling to myself.

19

My mind is filled with happy memories of Tasha and our beautiful bond. If I had not gathered courage and confronted the family, this could have panned out very differently. Thank god for small mercies.

I will never forget Sam and Tasha's wedding. Though the situation wasn't a smooth sail, the wedding was amazing. There were a few awkward moments when relatives asked about Drew, but we stuck to the same answer, "He was called away for his job immediately. They threatened to terminate his appointment if he did not join work, asap."

The relatives found the excuse unbelievable, but they kept mum nevertheless. But other than those trivial moments, the wedding was a runaway success. The pretty clothes, perfume engulfing the atmosphere, the food, the music and the vivacity was amazing. The chirpiness of the youth and the gathering of the entire clan was terrific.

Tasha looked like a princess. As for Sammy, I would never have guessed my brother could look so handsome. I saw a charming and caring side of him which Tasha always insisted he has, but I as a sister never saw. But since then I have seen many different sides of Sam. His magnified concern and care for Tasha after almost losing her. Marriage sure suits him and now fatherhood will too.

The end of the wedding brought a month-long honeymoon, leaving me with a lot of 'me-time'. During that period, I formulated the idea for my Café Library.

I worked on my ideas day and night to have my project ready to show dad. Dad not only approved, but helped me with the finer details. You remember Zoonie, don't you? She is an architect, whom I consulted to work with on my project.

I still remember when we met at our favourite food joint close to the college. It brought so much joy! The pranks we pulled, the fights, OMG. It all seems so silly now as we laugh over *the fight*, but yes, it did bring us all together. All five of us (Tasha included) meet once a year when Maya and Pearl are in town. The ruckus we create is unimaginable.

After hours of talking, I told her about my idea. I shared my vision, describing my dream intricately to her. I respected her for not asking me about Drew. Of course, word had spread. She must be aware of the gossip, but seeing me move beyond it all, she didn't bring the topic up.

She loved the whole concept of having a café attached to a huge library. I chuckled as I saw a different Zoonie with her work mode on. During college, I never noticed how extremely sharp and intelligent she was. But seeing her now not only impressed me, but inspired me too. She spoke in a plain business-like tone when she heard my idea,

"Kaira, I love the idea, but how do you plan to make this happen? Do you have a place decided for your cafe? Then there is the registration for your Café Library concept and the name for it? Have you thought of a name for it? Who do you plan to get it constructed by? Hey, the biggest and most important question – where is the money? From where and how are you planning to arrange money for such a huge project?"

Now, it was not easy to stun me, but she surely succeeded. I sat there looking at her with sheer amazement and silent respect. This was the same girl who hated books, was always the first to bunk classes and party all the time. Seeing this side of her made me miss the other one. But I knew that too existed.

I replied to her questions , "Wow, finally I get to put in a word! I would have shown you all the details had you waited a moment. But as it turns out, you have become just like me, impatient and impulsive. Lol!"

"Oh, okay! I got a little carried away. I loved the idea and the whole concept. So, speak up and show me what you got, baby!"

"So, our old Zoonie is still alive, eh? For a second there I felt that the face, voice and body are hers, but she seemed lost beneath this sophisticated costume."

I winked at her as she playfully whacked me in the head. "Okay, remember the small school building in Juhu, that has been shut down for years? The one right on the beach, behind the 5-star hotel?"

"Yes, I do! As a matter of fact, I am working on a deal with the owners to buy it for my company."

"No. You are kidding me! That is where I want to set up my Café Library. It is the perfect place. It's in a prime location, close to schools, colleges and even a few offices. Prithvi Theatre is nearby and the Juhu beach has an influx of thousands of people every day. The building is away from the traffic, more towards the beach and thus, it's the perfect spot."

"Amazing! You have really done your research. I am impressed! Since when have you been working on this?"

"Well, I have been on it since a few years now. In fact, I met with Mrs Choksi, the landlady, with my idea. She loved the concept and was ready to do business. Her asking price was astronomical, as it's prime property and in the heart of Mumbai. I could not have paid for it even if I took a loan and liquidated my assets. And then, as you know, I got distracted and..."

Zoonie looked at me pensively and spoke slowly, "Hmm, I understand. She mentioned a prospective buyer, it must be you! As my team couldn't find anyone."

"OMG! Imagine the probability of us both offering a buying price for the same property, huh?"

She was taken aback slightly, "What do you mean?"

I cleared my throat nervously and continued speaking, "Actually babe, there was a special reason I wanted to meet you today. Among all your questions, there was one about how will this dream come true? Well, I want you to help me with it. I can express my ideas, find the people, procure the books and set it up and run it. But the only person who can make my dream a reality is you."

She looked utterly surprised, my eyes brimming with sincerity. But I knew the concept had ignited a spark of excitement within her. I nervously awaited her response, knowing it was not a small monetary investment that I was asking of her. After the longest sixty seconds of my life, she exclaimed excitedly, "Yeeeessss, I would love to do this. In fact, I want to do it! From what you told me, it will be exciting and challenging. Mumbai's fast-paced life needs a quiet haven like this. The idea is a super hit!"

She sprang out of her couch and pulled me up to hug me tightly. I hugged her back with excitement, joy and relief. Suddenly she pulled back, "Hey, there is one problem. I will need a proper business proposal to present to dad. You need to whip up all the required investments, revenue details, presentation of charts, designs, layouts, also a possible profit graph. I will need you to impress him with limitless potential to this venture."

"Sweetheart, I have it all here." I give her the file from the chair beside me

"Oh my god! Babe, you have not only impressed, but shocked me today! Okay, first let me see your proposal before I say further."

She almost snatched the file from my hand and plonked herself on the couch. I sat quietly, watching her go through each sheet carefully. I saw her scribbling notes with a pencil every once in a while. Her thoroughness made me nervous and sweaty. I kept looking at her, twitching uncomfortably whenever she made notes.

The intensity in those black, beady eyes staring at me made me nervous and twitchy, till I lost patience.

"WTF Zoonie! Don't use your business tactics on me. You may be an astute businesswoman, but you, little miss, are still my friend. So, speak up! What do you think?"

Instead, she looked down and continued browsing through the file. She sure had mastered her father's art of keeping people on tenterhooks. I was feeling faint with the speed at which blood was rushing through my veins. Finally, she spoke, "This is excellent work Kai! So well-written and detailed. Yes, there are a few things we could work on, but even in its present form, it will leave an impact on my dad."

I gasped excitedly and clasped her hands, "Soooooo, that means you are on it with me!! Yay!!!"

She exclaims laughingly, "Ohhh babe, try stopping me now! But will it be in partnership or…?"

"Of course, I want to be the sole proprietor, but I would also be happy to have you as a sleeping partner in my dream venture. The profits can be split in 75/25, if it suits you and uncle."

She smiled mysteriously and said, "Hmm, let me speak to dad first. But I think we could work on the ratio once the finance team gets involved. One thing is for sure, we are doing this. It is a path-breaking idea that will change the way people read and interact in a busy city like Mumbai. If we adopt the franchisee format, we can replicate it across the country. Dad loves scalable projects; it makes him feel powerful. Hmm… where did you get this fabulous idea from?"

"Well, by sitting here, in this coffee shop."

"Huh? Explain..."

"Remember we spent most of our time here, especially during exams or assignment submissions. So, while I waited for you guys, I would hope they had books around to help pass the time. So, I did an in-depth study during our second year, and used this idea I had of having a café attached to a huge library for my thesis. Our English teacher loved the idea; in fact, she insisted on me doing a diploma in business too. Armed with all that, here I am."

"It's a unique idea; if it works then we will give Starbucks a run for their money. The idea of having educational books is superb; it will attract a lot of school students and youth. The idea of the project corner with research volunteers is phenomenal. You know, studying or reading with coffee and snacks close at hand, amazing. In the digital era where reading hard copies is disappearing, this concept will allow spaces for reading, encourage offline discussions and give a platform for intellectual expression. Wow! Simply wow!"

I beamed back with a smile that made my cheeks hurt. Yes! Finally, it looked like my dream would come true! I looked at Zoonie with a myriad of emotions and gratitude shining through my eyes. I continued softly, "So, you will talk to uncle, right? Ummn… When?"

"Today itself babe! In fact, I should be going now, I need to see him before he leaves for the US trip this week. Babe, start looking for the right kind of café staff, accountant, librarian, etc. Also start shortlisting the books that you wish to procure. Think about the décor, accounting system, cataloguing system and marketing, etc. Basically, everything that you will need to start. And hopefully, I should have his approval in a few days, max three."

We stood as she prepared to leave. Just before she sat in the car, I hugged her tightly once again and whispered softly in her ears, "Thanks a lot. This means a lot."

I was finally going to watch my dream manifest into reality.

20

I reached home with a spring in my step. The excitement of seeing my dreams turn into reality was immense. The past few weeks had been tough, but bouncing back strongly felt awesome.

On reaching home, I updated mom and dad on my meeting. I saw varied emotions on both their faces. One had love, pride and encouragement, the other was filled with fear, worry and concern – dad was apprehensive at the speed of it all. Both wanted me to think carefully before taking the leap. But I looked them in the eye with confidence and said, "Mom, Dad, I know I have made some rash decisions in the past. In fact, I have misused the liberty and freedom given to me. But this is not something I am doing impulsively. You both are aware of the fact that I have been working on this for a long time. My meeting Zoonie was to show how serious I am. Secondly, Zoonie is a businesswoman and a friend who will keep me grounded. She will not allow me to go beyond my capabilities."

As I awaited their decision, mom let out a long, heavy sigh of acceptance, but dad stared me down before announcing "Okay, Kaira. We give you one year to prove your potential. If by the end of next year, you don't prove yourself, I will get you married."

Fear rushed down my spine at the seriousness of his look and words. I saw the disappointment, hurt and humiliation I had caused him. His trust in me was shaken badly, for which I couldn't blame anyone but myself. But that one look also strengthened my resolve to make a success of this venture and prove to him that his faith in me was not wrong. But for now, I just hung my head down and accepted his conditions. "Thanks, Dad. I know I have disappointed you, but I will prove that I am your good daughter. I will gain that trust and pride back. I promise."

He didn't say anything, but just as he reached the bedroom door, he turned around and said, "All the best, my dearest daughter. I too want to see you succeed. I love you."

My eyes are bright with tears of regret even as he gives me his love and a second chance. The next few days, I waited eagerly for Zoonie's call. My entire future depended on this call. Even though mom offered all the love and support, she couldn't stop my heart skip a beat every time the phone rang.

Three days of waiting on pins and needles, I got *the* call. Dad was suggesting other possibilities as I lamented over my fate when the bell rang. Even though I had been awaiting it, the voice on the other end stunned me. Seeing my zapped state, mom and dad sat up straight. I didn't realize the call had ended, nor that the phone had slipped from my hand. I looked shocked. Mom got up to hug me and Dad said, "Sweetheart, was that Zoonie? Baby, it is going to be okay. We will figure another way to arrange finance. Don't get disheartened. Come on, child, it will all be fine."

It took me another few seconds to grasp the fact that they were upset for me. I shook myself out of my stupor and shouted, "Dad! Mom! It is fantastic news! Yes, that was Zoonie, her dad has agreed to my project, to my Café Library. Dad, my dream is going to be a reality."

Shouting this, I started jumping like a maniac. It took both mom and dad to hold me in tight hugs to calm me down. I hugged them back and suddenly started sobbing like a baby. They both stood by me as I wept long and hard.

After Drew's incident, deep down, I wasn't sure I would be able to pull this off. But now, with a confirmation in hand, I felt an adrenaline rush making me dizzy with sheer joy. Drew was my learning curve. Many girls experience similar situations, but not all are able to propel forward in life. I was being given a chance to prove myself to my family and make my dream come true. This was an opportunity for me to move forward in life.

I agreed to meet Zoonie at her office the next day. Having met her father a few times earlier, I bowed down and paid regards to him.

"Good morning uncle. How are you doing?"

Now Zoonie's father was a shrewd businessman. I had seen him in action once when I was at their home. He was very clear in his views and saw time as an investment. He therefore kept his conversations brief and to the point, especially if they were not marching towards evident profit. So, I knew him being here meant something important was to happen.

"Hello Kaira, I am doing very well. And from what I have seen, you have been working hard."

I avoided the urge to shuffle my feet nervously and blurted out, "I am trying, uncle."

He reiterated in an encouraging tone, "No, my child! I am really impressed with your project. Your detailing is very precise and the backward integration to profit margins is superlative. Everything was well-aligned and properly articulated. But now, I want you to show me your picture."

I looked at him, puzzled, "I am so sorry, uncle, but I don't understand what you're asking for."

He was holding my file in hand when he says, "Child, this is all on paper. I want to hear and see your vision. I want to understand your dream."

I understood what he meant. He was testing my passion. It reminded me of how he had spoken to his colleague a few years ago. His classic style was starting off by being friendly and then shaking that man's foundation with tricky questions that forced him to falter. Well, his style won't work with me. I not only knew my dream, but had been living with it for years now.

"Well, uncle, in that case, we need to go where my dream is going to manifest into reality."

My answer surprised him, but he agreed to go with me. The site was twenty minutes from their office. During the journey, he asked many questions, seeking details. He didn't say much, but listened and watched me like a hawk. A few times during the questioning, I looked at Zoonie for help, but she just smiled in encouragement.

When we reached the site, I felt excitement run through me. My eyes sparkled with joy; uncle noticed this too. I circled around the place, imagining how it would all look. For a minute I forget about uncle and Zoonie, until his cough for attention woke me to them.

I smiled sheepishly and say, "Ohhh, I am so sorry. I just got carried away."

He smiled back and said calmly, "I could see that. Now that you have us here, let's see how you plan to execute your vision."

About twenty-five minutes through my talk, I mentioned the corner for project mentors and also spoke of how ideas could be incubated here. Uncle's plastic smile changed to a warm and accepting one. I was guessing that my innovative initiatives and intricate details impressed him. At the end, I let out a long sigh of relief. I had a feeling that the company would back me and he would bless us. I saw pride and respect in his eyes, which made me feel an inch taller.

"Kaira, Zoonie, as they say, great initiatives and ideas are born twice, once in the mind and second in reality. I could see everything, every door, every window, even the chairs as you described. So, child, welcome aboard! You have my approval for this innovative project. I also agree with the 75/25 partnership, only because I see your hard work in putting this project together. I would love to see your vision come alive because it is beautifully articulated. However, I have one condition – we will be together for the franchise model as well. Hope you are okay with that?"

Instead of shaking uncle's hand, I touched his feet for blessings. This pleasantly surprised him; he put his hand on my head and quietly said, "God bless you."

We returned to the office to sign the papers and sealed the deal. Once done, I was getting ready to leave when Zoonie asked for a name.

"I am calling it Epistemic Cafe Library, which means relating to knowledge or the conditions to acquiring it, ECL in short."

"Wow, you really have thought everything through. I like the name, it's different. Hey, when is Tasha back?"

"Oh, it's just been a week since they left. Another three weeks or so. In fact, she called yesterday, and I told her about our agreement. She was ecstatic."

"Wow, how will she stay still now? She must be dying to get here and help."

"Oh, I'm sure Sam will keep her busy. Lol, and anyway, I have told her to rest and chill. She will be getting very busy with the interiors when she returns."

I called mom and dad with the good news. Dad sounded very happy, but the tone I wanted to hear was still missing. But I knew it won't be for long. Soon, I would earn the pride I used to hear in his voice.

While I awaited the blueprints, I met with Mrs Choksi for the finalization of the sale deed. The speed that money lends you is amazing! Things now moved at an unimaginable pace. Within two weeks, the building repairs started.

Once I agreed to the designs, Zoonie started the structural construction of the library. At the same time, I started looking for book wholesalers and publishing houses for educational books, novels, bestsellers, magazines, etc. Between it all, I also searched for people willing to help build the perfect cafe. People who were efficient at administration, accounting, cataloguing, cooking and marketing, among other profiles.

But finding the right people was a tough job. Recruiters charged a hefty commission, and despite that, the few they sent for an interview were unsuitable. We had time, so I kept my patience intact. The construction and repair work would need two months and another month for the detailing like light, water and electric points. After this, we would begin the interiors, that would take another month. So, I kept looking and waiting for Tasha, whose help I desperately needed now.

21

"Hey, are you thinking of Mystery Man again?"

The sound of Tasha's voice brings me back to the present. My eyes first go to the cradle to check on Angel and then to Tasha. She is eyeing me with a cheeky look.

"Good afternoon sleepyhead! How are you feeling?"

"I am feeling fine and rested, but you seemed far away."

"Hmm, delving into the past does that to you. Since yesterday, the past has been biting my ass at odd times."

She winks and jokingly remarks, "Hmm… you must be sore by now."

"Hahaha, you are funny! Anyway, do you want anything?"

Before she can answer, the nurse comes in with a snack. Well, lucky mommy being served while the attendant starves, huh! While I gather my thoughts, the door opens to let mom in.

"Hey mom, aren't you back early?"

"Kai, have you seen the time? It's 6 p.m.! In fact, everyone will be here soon. Which world are you living in?"

She shrugs and moves to Tasha after caressing Angel's pretty forehead. She calls over her shoulder, "There are some sandwiches and rolls in that bag. I know you must be hungry."

"Thanks mom, you are the best! I am really hungry."

While everyone is there, I ask, "Family, can I have your attention please?"

Hearing this, Sam blurts out, "Kai, can you cut down your dramatics? Talk like a normal person for a change."

I frown at him and reply, "Ya, I can see you missed me. I know everyone is busy with Angel, but can you all please decide on a name?"

I turn away from him and look at the rest.

"I know I sound pushy, but I need a proper name for this cutie, even though Angel sounds nice."

"Kai, we like the name Arshi. It is short, sweet and meaningful."

Mala aunty rarely makes announcements or decisions in the family, so it comes as a pleasant surprise.

Everyone nods in consent. I gleefully clap my hands and walk towards mom. She is holding Arshi in her arms. I touch the baby's face lightly and whisper softly in her ears, "Welcome to our crazy family, Arshi." I plant a peck on her forehead and look up to find everyone busy talking among themselves.

"Mom, when is Tasha going to be discharged? Just asking cos I won't be able to come to the hospital tomorrow."

"I think she will be discharged the day after tomorrow, depending on her stitches. As for tomorrow, it's okay as I am coming home tonight. Mala will be staying with Tasha tonight and I will stay tomorrow afternoon. If you want to leave even now, you can."

I kiss Arshi again, wish everyone goodbye as I leave. I ignore Drew, even though I notice him stealing looks at me. Don't you find his behaviour odd? Hmm… I wonder why!

I am just about to start my bike when my cell phone rings. This invention is the best way to invade privacy. Sure, they are convenient and handy, but they almost always ring at the wrong time. But it's the Café. As soon as I answer the phone, a voice rambles at the other end,

"Sorry for troubling you at this late hour, but I just had to remind you of your meeting tomorrow at noon with the devil."

I smile and reply, "Well, hello to you to Nikita. I am well, and so are Tasha and Arshi. Yes, we have finally named Angel. Isn't it a lovely name… Arshi?"

Nikki sighs and apologetically continues speaking, "Okay, okay! I am sorry! But that man has me at my wit's ends. I don't want anything to go wrong tomorrow. I don't want to give him the opportunity to label me as an inefficient member of ECL."

I sigh in exasperation, "Relax, will you? You are stressing me out as well! I will be in at 11 a.m., so chillax for now. Now I gtg… bye!"

Good heavens, who is this Aveer Mehra? I Googled him the other day again; there is a lot about his achievements but no photograph. The articles praise his professional contribution, but nothing about him or his personal life. Is he really as bad as Nikki portrays him to be? Well, time will tell. Right now, all I need is my bed.

During the ride home, my mind wanders to the thoughts of *my* Mystery Man. Hmm… strange! Since when did I start thinking of him as mine now… huh!

I don't even think we will meet again, even though destiny crossed our paths twice! And each time, he made me feel nice about myself. Yes, I appear to be a successful extrovert, but deep inside, I am still emotionally scarred, who had closed all doors to relations. I still make friends with boys, but have never got involved with anyone again. The past has been hard to let go of, but Mystery Man opened the floodgates of my heart. How? I am not sure. A car honk close to me shakes me up.

Oops! I am being careless, again. I better concentrate on the road.

I see a note stuck on the door of my house. I open the envelope and burst out laughing till tears run down my happy face. I shake my head exclaiming, "Nikki, Nikki! What has this devil done to you?" Wait a minute! Did I just label the man as the devil? Gosh! He seems to be getting into my head too!

I read the note again, 'Kai, call me paranoid, stupid or whatever adjective you come up with. But please be on time. I don't want to have to deal with the devil again please. XOXO.'

Wow, I am intrigued! I remember when Nikki had first come for an interview three-and-a-half years ago. She was unemployed and inexperienced. It was her commendable risk-taking appetite and the go-getter attitude that had impressed me. Over the years, she turned out to be ECL's biggest asset. Later she confessed that my positivity and confidence instilled faith in her. She could relate to my vision the same way I did to her dreams.

She became my Lady Friday (if there exists a term like that!). She got involved with every aspect of operations and allowed me to focus on other crucial ones.

Zoonie, Tasha, Nikita and I could plan the interiors, the furniture for the books and our office space. But running a fully functional café that serves good food and drinks needed the handiwork of an expert.

Good food and coffee would make my library even more welcoming. We tried poaching, recruitment firms and college drives, but came back empty-handed. This worried me to no end.

We almost gave up and thought of tying up with a third party, when I accidentally met Robin and Pete.

We happened to be at the same coffee shop. I was waiting for the interviewee and they, for their interviewer.

They mistook me for their interviewer and we got talking. We just struck a wonderful rapport.

It's only when my interviewee, the gourmet chef, approached our table did we realize the case of mistaken identity. But we didn't see the need to rectify it.

They had agreed to all the terms. I liked them, they seemed experienced, aware and committed. They had the enthusiasm to explore a different terrain. Something I appreciated and wanted.

The next day, during the tasting session, we were greeted with a wide array of the most scrumptious food. The table was laid out with a wide variety of pastries, puffs, sandwiches and the best coffee ever. You already know about my romance with coffee; so, when I say it was the best, of course I am right!

Robin and Pete had turned coffee making into a science of personality typing. They had a flavour for every person according to their outlook and personality. This innovation brought us a lot of accolades later. I was on a roll. ECL now had everything to get started. The library almost ready, the café was in the process, books were set for display, the décor was complete, and to top it, we had the best staff ever. Though different, we were all united by a common vision that allowed us to form a relationship beyond work. ECL was now all set and my extended family was ready to conquer Mumbai!

22

I smile at the memories as I set aside Nikki's note. Mom has cooked and stored the food in the fridge. I pile my plate with food and plonk myself on the sofa in front of the television. As I enjoy the soulful food, I savour the fruits of my success and being blessed to share it with like-minded people.

Zoonie, Tasha, Nikita, Robin, Pete and I – we were the perfect team. It took a little longer than we anticipated, but finally, ECL was ready for business. I still get the jitters as I remember the excitement among readers, the excited questions from the journalists. Zoonie's dad's PR agency did wonders for the launch. ECL was established as a popular youth hangout, and yes, we were here to stay.

I take a deep breath and loudly mutter to myself, "Enough Kaira! I think you have wasted enough time reminiscing the past. Enough is enough. The past should be left where it's supposed to be – in the past. Sleep now, if you want to be at ECL on time tomorrow morning."

The minute my head touches the pillow, I drift off to sleep. Immediately, I am back by the road with Mystery Man's arms around me. As I look at him, I watch the colours changing in his eyes. I see concern turn to such intense passion that I tremble in my sleep. He pulls me closer, strengthening his grip around my waist. I see his handsome face slowly move close to mine. Time seems to stop. I see rainbows in the sky, clouds surround us in a small world of our own. I can feel his warm breath on my quivering ones. I wet my dry lips just a few seconds before his touch mine, a shiver so strong shakes my whole body, making me pull back an inch.

As our breaths mingle, I feel as if my soul is getting merged with his. His lips are close to mine, just a few millimetres away; they do not touch mine again. He runs his gaze all over my face while I look deep into his eyes, waiting; he stays still. He keeps looking at me lovingly; we seem frozen in time.

"Why… what... why…?" I whisper softly.

He opens his mouth when a shrill noise shatters the moment.

It is my alarm… Urrgh!!

Shit! Did I just get kissed by a stranger in my dreams? Was I asking him why was he waiting? Why am I so upset – because of the dream or because he did not complete the kiss? Shucks! What is wrong with me?

I drag myself out of bed and get ready to meet the devil. Good lord! I need to stop biasing myself against Mr Aveer, lest it reflects in our meeting.

I slip into my favourite jeans with a white top and sweeping my hair into a smart, high pony and spritz my favourite perfume. I team my outfit with these gorgeous hoop earrings that I had picked up at the flea market last week. I quickly wear my beige espadrille, which are trendy and most comfortable, especially for the cafe. Now, make-up and I are always at loggerheads. But today, I had to concede. Gosh! This deal better be worth all the extra effort! Mom and dad are having breakfast, talking softly among themselves. I stand by the door, wishing I too had someone to share my most insignificant thoughts with. It must be so amazing to share this kind of camaraderie and mutual respect with someone, like them. A relation where you can discuss anything and share loving moments without being conscious of people around. As kids, we have seen them fight like enemies and make up as best friends do. It seems like a distant dream for me, or does it? Huh!

"Good morning lovebirds. May I join in?"

"Kai, behave yourself! You still are our daughter, so please show due respect and manners."

Dad's booming voice reminds me of my Mystery Man's tone. Our first encounter? Gosh! Am I going crazy? Shit, *him* again. I turn red in the face. I sheepishly look at mom… Shoot! She knows something is odd. She always knows, but she always waits.

"Mom, can you please make some coffee for me? I really have to rush. Your coffee is my lucky charm… always, whereas mine could kill the dead!"

I send her a flying kiss as she goes to the kitchen.

I sit with dad while he is engrossed in his morning newspaper. "Kai, who is the devil?"

I feel my stomach turning. Luckily, I am not holding or drinking anything. I surely would have dropped it or choked on it.

I swing my gaze from dad to mom and then back to dad. He was holding Nikki's note.

I heaved a sigh of relief. "Oh, that! I don't know dad. I have yet to meet the man who Nikita has tagged as the devil. All I know is that his name is Aveer Mehra. I had mentioned him some time back."

Dad blinks for a few seconds and suddenly remembers, "Yes, yes, hmm, well what about him?"

"I was to meet him the day before yesterday. But had to take a rain check due to Tasha's delivery. I left it to Nikki to deal with him, to which he took offence. He brushed her aside and I think was rude to her as well. So, she has been jittery ever since."

Dad looks at me pensively, "So what are you going to do about it? If I remember correctly, you said you were expecting huge business from him."

I reply like a rebellious schoolgirl who was being questioned by the principal.

"It is dad, I agree. I may, I repeat, I may make some money and get a good collection of books from him. But if he is rude, especially with the staff, then there is no place for him in ECL."

Dad ignores my indignant behaviour and replies, "Kai, please think calmly and maintain the dignity of your status. Before reacting, hear both sides of the story. Always remember, a little diplomacy is always good for business."

I nod in agreement. I know what he means and somewhere deep down, I agree with his hunch. By now even you know me, I don't think before I act. I quickly finish my coffee and dash out of the door.

I check my watch; it is only 9.30 a.m., and the meeting is at noon. I have enough time to catch up with my pending chores at work, especially organising the new books I had ordered. Did I mention how I love organizing bookshelves?

The feel of holding books is incredible. Any fan of books will swear by the wondrous smell of books. It gives me a high that is difficult to spell in words. Books have kept me company ever since I remember. There is a book to suit every person, mood and occasion. While organizing books, I sometimes leaf through the pages to get a glimpse of what the book offers.

23

I look out at the sea from the parapet outside the cafe. I watch the waves romancing the soft sands. I breathe in the salty air and smile. What a beautiful day it is! The café is bustling with the early morning crowd making a beeline for our breakfast specials. The library is already full of people; studying, reading novels, writing journals or typing away at their laptops. Some office-goers are either giving last minute touches to a presentation or replying to emails.

I look around and take a deep breath at the Epistemic Cafe Library, fondly called as ECL. It's my sanctuary, my dream come true.

Zoonie's architectural prowess allowed the design to retain the high ceilings that she converted to skylights. The huge French windows ensured that readers can soak in the beauty of the Arabian Sea. There is natural light coming in from all sides of ECL. From every corner here, the world seems to be a better place. The place has no ceilings, just glass all round and above.

Zoonie gave us sliding doors facing the beach, with comfortable outdoor seating options.

The most attractive part of my place is the centre area. It is constructed in an oval shape open to the sky. We replaced the cemented roof with solid waterproof toughened glass fittings that housed beautiful chandeliers emitting white light.

People always feel one with nature at my Café. It is a sight to behold, especially during the rains. The Café is frequented by young lovebirds who enjoy the pitter-patter of raindrops while watching the waves of the sea playing with the sand. It almost feels like playing in the rain without getting wet. It is beautiful and surreal.

Zoonie was very particular about the maintenance and upkeep, so ECL always looks as good as new.

Robin and Pete created a perfect haven for foodies. And their innovative recipes allow patrons to explore tastes and tickle their palates. Robin would use his skills to whip up customized dishes as per a patron's mood and that became a runaway hit among patrons. The top floor houses my dream world, my library. No one can guess looking at the place that it stores more than one lakh books. The books are placed in the form of steps with a place for one to climb, the ladders help patrons to reach specially positioned rare books. I have divided the books into sections as per the requirements of readers. Nikki has catalogued all the books as per their placement, and with precision. It is extremely easy to locate books, especially those placed higher up.

I placed all the chairs and tables around the centre area. Even the library area opens to the beach. Every corner and window has open cupboards with more books. We have stocked regular stationery for students, just to make things easier for them.

It is a paradise for any and every kind of patron, and it is *my paradise.* In the beginning, I used to practically live here. Many a time, you can find me napping in one of the balconies. What made me feel on top of the world was the pride I saw in my parents' eyes when they first saw the Café. We received compliments from everyone, including Zoonie's father. He especially cornered dad to applaud my success.

With time, our standards have risen, and the processes have been perfected. For more financial benefits, on several occasions, we opened the café for small gatherings and celebrations. We recently added a new member to our team, Anita, who helps in the cafe part-time. At other times, she studies for her Master's at ECL.

ECL has grown to become a way of life for many. People of all ages and groups are seen here. From a mother who is teaching her 2-year-old to read to an eighty-year-old enjoying coffee/tea while reading by the beach. Corporates have used our spaces for informal conferences and meetings. Authors for reading sessions. ECL resonates with happiness that is housed within the silent hearts of its patrons.

24

Whenever I enter ECL, a wave of joy passes through my body. The feelings of humble pride and satisfaction is always endearing. This is my perfect home away from home.

"Hello people! How is everyone doing today?"

"Good morning, Kai! How would you like your coffee today? I would say a Mocha Latte with caramel sauce would be just perfect…eh?"

"Ohh Pete! You are the best. How do you guess the right flavour each time?" I wink at him and smile encouragingly.

Robin is attending to hungry customers, so I just wave at him. Anita is behind the counter taking orders, so she just raises her hand and smiles briefly. I look around for my drama queen. I spot her staring at the blank computer screen, so I quietly go to her.

"Good morning Nikki, my new drama queen! How are you this morning?"

She yelps in surprise while placing her hand on her chest. She looks at me in shock.

"Like really, Kai! I could have had a heart attack. I am already nervous, so don't scare me. And what do you mean by 'drama queen'?"

"What else should I call you? This thing you have been harping about, it is so unlike you. You have been behaving weirdly ever since you met Aveer Mehra. So now tell me what the issue is?"

Her expressions make me even more curious. There must be something more to this story.

"Look Kai, whatever I told you is true. Mr Mehra was rude and insulting, but in a very polite manner. Like a sweet knife that can kill you when you least expect it."

"Wow! Fab metaphor!"

She gives me a dirty look and continues, "I was completely in awe of his killer looks as well. He really is the most handsome devil I have ever seen. Dresses immaculately in a nice Armani suit, polished and aristocratic. His panache made me go weak in the knees. So, to be brushed aside albeit respectfully by such a handsome looking man was embarrassing."

"I thought it was a Prada..." I speak distractedly.

But when I refocus on Nikki, I see her give me a killer look and her face turns a beautiful shade of red. She seems completely besotted! Dad was right and I am glad I speak to Nikki before I act at the meeting.

"OMG! You have a crush on Mr Aveer Mehra. This isn't anger at all. I was right! You are a drama queen! What about Sunny? You do remember him? Sunny, your fiancé... huh?"

She wrings her hands nervously, "Shut up, Kai! Of course, I remember Sunny. I love him a lot. But which book preaches that I cannot appreciate another man while being in a relationship!"

"Gosh! You make him sound like a Greek god! I can't wait to see what all the huu-haa is about. But right now, how about we finish some important work instead of this mindless chatter?"

Nikki looks at me guiltily and gets the files for my perusal. As we tally the accounts, I remember about the new books that were to arrive.

"Hey Nikki, did those books we ordered from High Book publishers arrive?"

She nods affirmatively.

"Yes Kai. I have catalogued and arranged them according to the sections. So that it will be easy for you to put them up."

"Thanks a ton; you are an angel! I am glad you hate heights, or you would have done my favourite job of putting them on the shelves too."

We finish our work and Nikki goes back to her desk. "Okay with this done, I am going to arrange the books on the shelf. Where are they?"

"But Kai, there are at least a hundred books and all to be placed in different sections. It will take at least an hour to finish. The devil will be here in about twenty minutes. Also, your clothes will get soiled and that won't look good. It's a professional meeting after all—"

"Gosh Nikki! Please get a grip and stop making a big deal about him. I will be quick. Even if he is here, my chores shouldn't bother him. If he really is a workaholic, he will appreciate other's commitment too. As for my clothes, any dust can be brushed off. I am not going to stop working because of some specks of dirt."

I take a few books and start climbing the ladder. Halfway through, I plug in my earphones, switch on my favourite set music and get to work. The flow of music fills me with energy.

I start from the top and arrange the books meticulously beside each other. I feel someone standing near my feet. I call out without looking, "Hey Nikki, hand me the last lot. I am almost done here. Oh btw, has the Devil arrived? You said he was a stickler for perfection and punctuality—" While examining the shelf, I absentmindedly stretch out my hand and say, "Give the books, fast… and yes, I really need to stop calling him the devil… what if I say that to his face? God.... now, that would be embarrassing! You know Nikki, the other day…"

I keep talking and swaying to the music while making space for the books with one hand, my other still outstretched. But instead of a book, a warm but seemingly familiar hand holds mine.

I try pulling back my hand as I look down surprised, shoot! I am looking straight into my Mystery Man's eyes. This must be a dream! I tug at my hand, but he just tightens his hold. Another hard tug and I lose my balance and topple down the ladder. This scene is straight out of a Bollywood film! But this time, I am sure that I would be safe. Yes, I find myself snugly placed in my Mystery Man's arms. Oh...!!

25

"Ms Fireball, we should stop meeting like this! I just might start believing that you keep falling into my arms on purpose!"

Huh, what the heck! What is he doing here? As usual, he is turning the tables onto me. I haven't even spoken a word!

Silence is an alien quality to me, yet, every time I meet him, I am tongue-tied.

I open my mouth in protest, but his eyes..., oh his soulful eyes, they shut my mind off. To top it, he fixes his loving gaze on my face. My heart is pounding in excitement, my throat is parched, and my mind is reeling. And in all this, I am feeling happy. Uff! What is happening… everything ceases to exist. I think even he can hear the loud beats of my heart because I see his eyes move down to stop at my heaving bosom. I feel my nipples harden at his glance and my breath nearly stops. I feel powerless. What on earth is happening to me?? Just when I think I am going to choke under the pressure of emotions surrounding us, Nikita calls out.

"Hey Kai, are you okay?"

I try talking, but no words come out. His eyes have arrested my entire being again. Nikki moves to my side, nearly shouting into my ear, "Kai, Kai talk to me babe!"

I emerge out of the emotional deluge and shake my head to get rid of the lustful feelings. My nipples are still hard as I give Mystery Man one last glance and then turn to Nikki.

"Ya, I am fine. Just lost my balance. Mister, you can put me down now, please."

I avoid looking into his eyes.

"Are you sure? Whenever I let you go, you vanish without a trace."

He is whispering into my ears, sending goose bumps through my body.

He carefully sets me down; my body slides against his while he does so. My body is warm, my cheeks are burning as my feet touch the ground. The thought of being away from him is killing me.

Beads of perspiration dot my eyebrows as I compose myself. Nikki keeps looking at me questioningly. To nail my coffin of embarrassment, I notice patrons staring at me, smiling slyly. I can feel strong vibes from the man standing too close for comfort. I clear my throat and say, "Okay guys, the show is over! Please, get back to your respective tasks."

I turn to my Mystery Man, gather courage and blurt out, "What are you doing here?"

He looks at me for a few seconds before saying, "Ohh, you are welcome. I am just glad I was there at the right time to save you... again."

I feel my forehead crinkle in response to his statement. What is he talking about? That's when realization hits me, "Ohhh, you want me to thank you for something you caused? I was up there, working peacefully, as soon as you entered, disaster struck. If it were not for your sudden appearance, I would have been just fine. So, you can wait till hell freezes before I say a thank you."

"God, Fireball! There you go again with your weird but loveable attitude! I must add, however, that whenever I meet you my day gets brighter. It's always an interesting story I can narrate to my friends."

"Hahahaa, I am glad at least one of us feels happy! Will you please answer my question?"

"Umm, which was…? Ohh yes! 'What am I doing here?' I could ask you the exact same thing."

I turn away from him and look at Nikita, who is still standing there, zapped.

"Nikki, please check if Mr Aveer has arrived. I really need to wrap up and go home."

I wait for her to move, but she just stands there. She keeps moving her eyes from Mystery Man to me, and back again. He smirks and chuckles. Shoot! Is he Aveer Mehra? Gosh! I guess he is! I curse myself and look around for an asylum. My Mystery Man is the devil? No! It is too much of a coincidence! Well, what can I say? My day just got more interesting.

I shake Nikki from her stupor. She finally looks at me and hurriedly says, "Ms Kaira, ma'am, this is…"

"Yes, I know! This is Mr Aveer Mehra, right?"

He chuckles and says, "I thought I was the devil."

I dart a dirty look towards him and turn to Nikki. She is recovering from her shock. I think she has caught a whiff of our chemistry. I will have to cook up an explanation later.

"Nikki, please request Robin to get some sandwiches and coffee for our guest. And while you are at it, please speak to the children who especially ordered these books to come and check if we ordered the right ones."

She nods and rambles, "Yes, yes ma'am… okay ma'am…!"

Did my Nikki just call me ma'am? Huh?

Oh god! What is the enchantment surrounding this man? My most competent friend is behaving like a confused teenager in his presence. I examine him with the corner of my eye. He stands upright, looking straight at me. When the silence gets deafening, he clears his throat and asks, "Okay Fireball, are you through or you want to ogle at me some more?"

I quickly respond, "Hmm, you are embarrassed and so you are trying to make me uncomfortable. Interesting, huh! I can't seem to figure out why my normally calm friend is so flustered in your presence."

He gapes at me in surprise. Nikki gasps as she hears me while entering the room. Good heavens! Not again!

"Nikki, how about you arrange the food outside?"

She looks at me apologetically and goes outside as instructed. What! She is a robot now? I motion to Aveer to follow me out. So, is a silly crush the only reason why Nikki seemed so offended earlier? Of course, Mr Aveer was good looking, but…

I offer Aveer a seat before joining him. He continues to watch me carefully and says, "I like you. No, I really do like you."

I feel a twang in my heart, as if a hundred violins are playing at the same time.

"Are you asking me or telling me? I like me too. And as much as I like being liked, you, Mister don't even know me. So…???"

He ignores my rant and continues, "You bring out something nice in me. Usually people get intimidated or are in awe of me. You argue and always put me in my place. It makes me want to continue ruffling your feathers."

"Well, you haven't succeeded as yet."

"Are you sure I haven't?"

I clear my throat and change the topic.

"Welcome to ECL, Mr Mehra. I am the owner, Ms Kaira Kapoor, you can call me Kaira."

I extend a handshake. He is surprised, but tactfully handles it.

"I thought I was the devil, wasn't I?"

"Okay, you were not supposed to hear that. I wasn't aware that you were around, else I would have restrained myself from saying those words. But then one very rarely hears good things about themselves behind their backs."

I can't resist needling him. He deserves it, doesn't he?

"Hmm, you may be right. But I need to know why I have been labelled as the devil, Ms Kaira."

Uff…he takes my name! My name sounds so much sweeter when he says it. My heart starts pounding again. I look him directly in the eye and reply, "Well, I didn't choose this label. I guess it chose you. You frightened Nikki like no one has ever done. Come to think of it, it seems to suit you."

It is as if our bodies are communicating on one plane, but our hearts are communicating on another. We look at each other in silence. The air is filled with mixed emotions. We both keep looking at each other, none of us ready to break free. We seem to be enjoying the undefined challenge between us. I don't know how long we would have continued if not for the ringing of my cell phone. I am forced to break eye contact to check who it is. It's just a number with no name. I put it on silent. I take a deep breath before looking at him again.

"Let's get down to business. I really have to rush."

"Hmm, if you don't mind my asking, where do you have to go?"

Should I share details of my personal life with him? Isn't it too early?

"I have to shop for my niece and prepare for her homecoming. There is a lot to do and very little time."

Shucks! What is wrong with me? I need to get my act together, like… *now!*

"In fact, I would have been shopping right now if it wasn't for an arrogant man who refused to deal with my second in command. He insisted on meeting only me!"

Instead of getting offended, he surprises me by laughing out loudly. Gosh! His laugh is cuter than him. I look at him with amazement as a smile graces my mouth too.

He smiles and remarks, "See, I told you I liked you and I was not wrong about it. Your forthright attitude impresses me. You not only made me feel like a pompous idiot, but made me feel guilty too. Very few people can do that and get away with it."

God… wt…

"I believe you. You can't be where you are without an ego and narcissism. As for making you feel guilty, that was not my intention. But if you are feeling guilty, then please be nice to my friend and restore her confidence."

"Hmm, I will see what I can do. But that day my mind was elsewhere, particularly on a crash with a live fireball. So, the heated attitude and arrogance was unintentional."

My mind jogs back to our first meeting. I pull myself together and straighten up. I was going to be late if this conversation continues like this.

"Mr Mehra, it's almost lunch time, would you like to grab something from our cafe?"

"Nope, I think we should get to work."

We pull our chairs close and study the files together. For the next hour, we both focus on work. He has excellent ideas for my business, but the pricing is a bit high. We argue and contradict for a while, and then finally find a middle path.

He finally agrees to send me the latest monthly catalogues. We get into a non-compete clause and seal the deal. The best part is that he agrees to display flexibility if he cannot arrange a book. Brainstorming and discussing with him is refreshing. We connect on so many levels. We both are stubborn, but fair in our respective fields. None is ready to compromise on values and principles. I like him. Hmm... doing business with him will be fun.

26

We are wrapping up when Nikki comes in with a tray full of food. Robin tags along, carrying the drinks. We are way past lunch time and seeing food makes me realize how hungry I am.

"I am blessed with friends like you, Robin and Nikki! How did you know I'm hungry?"

"Well, we have been working with you for four years now," a composed Nikki replies smilingly.

She looks at Aveer and remarks, "Hunger makes her irritable, so beware! You don't want to be a target of hypoglycemic rage… do you?"

"Hey, why are you telling him this? It is none of his business!"

But Nikki continues to look at Aveer. Their newfound camaraderie is making me uncomfortable. "What on earth is going on here?"

No one answers. Aveer continues to eye Nikki, his expressions go from bright to blank. Nikki keeps her gaze steady as if she is trying to tell him something. I look at Robin for help, but he shrugs his shoulders and leaves. I am about to lose my nerve when Aveer speaks, "Kaira is right. You are smart and intelligent. I can see why she trusts you so much. You are not only clever, but observant too, I appreciate that. And yes, I apologize for my behaviour the other day. It was very petty of me to have underestimated you. It is a blunder I won't make again."

Wow, what just happened here? What did that one look from Nikki say to Aveer? How did his stance change suddenly? He could have apologized plainly, but this was beyond my expectation.

"What the heck transpired here? Will you guys speak up?"

"Nothing much, Fireball. Your friend saw something that even I had not noticed. You are fortunate to have such an amazing friend in your team."

Wow! He is back to calling me Fireball, that too in front of Nikki. Wait a minute… Am I feeling jealous? Another alien emotion! Ohhh god! How much more is remaining for me to experience?

Even when I was crazy for Drew, I never once felt jealous when he was with another girl. But right this moment, when Nikki and Aveer seemed to have hit it well, I feel a twinge in my heart. I don't like this feeling. Feeling envy and jealousy is just not me!

I get up abruptly and say, "Aveer, since we have concluded the meeting, I need to rush. So, if you will excuse me, I will take your leave."

I ignore Nikki's looks and move towards the door when a hand stops me. It's Aveer, again.

"Hey, what about lunch? I thought you were hungry."

"Yes, I am, but I just saw the time. It is very late. Nikki can give you company… right Nikki?"

I rush out as if a rabid dog was pursuing me. I ignore the looks I get from Aveer and Nikki. I think Nikki was smiling cheekily. Was she?

I have just reached my bike when I feel the vibes once again. The familiar pounding of my heart has started again.

"What's wrong, Kaira?"

No! Don't call me by my name! I don't like this feeling of melting in your care. What? What am I saying? Ms Fireball or Kaira, call me anything you wish. I just don't care.

Gosh! This man has squeezed more emotions out of me in three freaking days than Drew had in all these years.

I look at him, like a forlorn lamb, confused and worried. He continues to look at me. Is that love I see in his eyes? No, it's my imagination. I don't want him to feel that I caused it. Later he will narrate this story to his friends saying that I came on to him, just like Drew.

The way he is looking at me is very different from how he looked at Nikki. This look has love, desire and care shining through. Maybe I am imagining all this. I unconsciously take a step back, only to be stopped by my bike.

His hands are resting on mine as he continues to stare silently. I unconsciously remove my tongue to wet my now dry lips. He groans softly at my unintentional sensual move. I shiver at the sound and look up to him. His eyes are on my wet lips.

Suddenly, Aveer pulls me towards him and places his lips on mine. The feel of him pecking at the wetness of my lips and then slowly nipping the corner of my mouth makes blood rush to my head. He slowly takes my lower lip between his teeth and playfully tugs at it. I want to stop him, but I can't, or should I say I don't want to. His lips feel like they were meant only to kiss me. The feel of his lips is different from Drew's. I feel an electric current run through my body. Aveer's kiss reaches my soul and touches it like no one has before. It's so sensuous, so soft that it feels like my very first kiss. My body is throbbing, and beads of perspiration run down my forehead. We are locked in a tight embrace. I never want to let go and so, I kiss him back. We are locked in a trance for several minutes.

I sigh deeply and sink into his protective arms. I lay my head on his chest for a while, and when I look up, we kiss again. My phone starts to vibrate after a while. I try stepping away from him, my gait unsteady, but he holds me, like always. With him around, I can never fall or falter.

I answer the phone, it's mom. I mumble a soft 'hello'. She does all the talking, I let her instruct me and reply in monosyllables. I disconnect her call and look into the eyes of the man who has shaken me to the core. His gaze is fixed on me. I blush and look away. My eyes travel to ECL's door… Shucks! Nikki had seen us. She smiles and gives me a thumbs up. Seeing my shattered look makes her worried.

She comes down to check on me. I clasp her hand for support. She pats my hand and turns to Aveer, "I think we should all call it a day. Why don't we fix an appointment for next week for the formalities?"

Aveer realizes we have crossed a line and looks embarrassed. He stands there waiting for me to say something. I avoid his gaze and mutter something to Nikki about leaving immediately from there. "Okay, I am leaving. You will hear from me soon. Take care and feel free to call me anytime, okay?"

I continue looking down and nod my head. He leaves quietly. From the corner of my eye, I watch him getting into his Mercedes.

My heart wants to scream, 'Stop, don't go Aveer!' But my mind stops me from doing so. Fear and insecurities of the past swamp me. I know he looks back one more time before he leaves, but I keep my gaze lowered and away.

27

For the first time, standing outside ECL is making me uncomfortable. It's nearly 4 p.m. and the sun is slowly losing its heat. The light breeze helps cool down a bit of my anxiety. I don't even realize that I am still squeezing Nikki's hand. She calls out to me a couple of times. I come back to reality feeling nervous, scared and unsure of myself. I look at Nikki with glazed eyes. She takes me back in.

I sit by the window trying to get a grip on myself. Robin gets a strong cup of coffee with a hint of cinnamon and honey. My friends gather around, worried about my well-being. Once I feel a little more like me, I look at them with grateful eyes. Once they are sure I am ok, Robin and Pete go back to the counter, but Nikki sits with me.

"You okay now?"

"Ya, I am better, but still can't understand what happened. One moment he was talking professionally, and the next, we are kissing passionately. How? For that matter, why?"

Nikki smiles reassuringly and says, "Sweetheart, don't question it. Just go with the flow. Time will tell."

"Have you exchanged souls with Tasha? Why are you talking like her? Anyway, I feel better now, thanks a ton. Gtg! I have lots to do."

Just as I reach the exit, I call out to them, "Hey guys, mom called to say that Tasha is back home tomorrow. There is a small get together for near and dear ones. You all are invited. Please close the cafe by 5 p.m. tomorrow and be on time."

"Kai, I know it is too early, but I have a suggestion. Why not invite Aveer for the family celebration tomorrow? Uncle and aunty will get to meet him, and he'll take the spotlight away from Drew."

"Are you crazy? Why would I do that? What will I tell my parents? And as for Drew, I can handle him. He doesn't matter in my life anymore. In fact, handling Aveer would be tougher."

"Listen sweetie, it is just a suggestion, rest is up to you. Think about it. Bye, see you tomorrow."

She goes back, but leaves me in a dilemma. I need to talk to Tasha asap. Instead of going to the market, I go to the hospital. I don't remember clearly how I make my way to the hospital. Once outside, I strain my ears to try and hear who all are in. The coast seems clear. I slowly open the door to find Mala aunty there. My eyes go to the bed, where Tasha is feeding Arshi.

"Hello, aunty… Hey mommy dear! How you and Angel doing?"

"I am doing good. I didn't think you were coming today. Mom said you had work at the Café and then shopping "

I avoid looking at her, "Ya, but I missed you and Angel. I could always shop later."

"Hmm…!?"

Shucks! She knows me well enough to catch my lie. Seeing my state, she asks Mala aunty to take a break as I am there with her. I don't hear aunty leave, so lost I am in thoughts. It isn't until Tasha practically shouts my name that I jerk back to the room. I look at her imploringly. Seeing the storm brewing in my eyes has her pulling me close. She softly asks me, "What happened, Kai?"

I burst into tears and narrate the entire story and start shivering when I describe the kiss.

Tasha reassures me by rubbing my hands softly.

After a while I look around, "Where is aunty?"

"Sweetheart, she left a while ago, much before you started speaking. You were too lost to notice."

"Shit! I hope I didn't scare her. I need to go call her, to reassure her that I am kk."

"Kai, don't worry, she will be back soon. But before that, I want to know what you plan to do about him."

"I don't know yet. Nikki says I should call him tomorrow for your homecoming party. But I don't want to be the first to call."

Someone up there must have been listening closely because the moment I say the words, my phone buzzes. I look at Tasha with surprise when I read the SMS. It is from him! I give her my phone to read,

'Hi, Fireball. I hope you doing kk. I am sorry. I should not have done what I did. I am sorry for scaring you, that was not my intention. It just happened. Please forgive me. Waiting to hear from you.'

Tasha sighs, "It is a little formal but cute. I think you should reply. I also think Nikki is right, calling him tomorrow is a good idea. That way, everyone gets to meet him and gauge if he is a good man. You know our parents have a sixth sense for us."

"But Tasha, under what pretext can I call him. He is still a stranger! I know nothing about him. What will I tell the parents? What should I tell him? It's too complicated babe."

"No, you are making it out to be. Just tell your dad you want to introduce him to a prospective client and want his opinion like always. We don't have to tell him that this client makes your heart beat faster or that he kissed our Sleeping Beauty and woke her up like the Prince, huh!"

"Hahaha, you are funny. Okay, let me think about it. Now I need to go, I have work to finish. Please tell me where you sent aunty?"

"Smart ass! She is right behind you!"

I turn to see aunty who has just entered. She looks at me carefully. Observing that I am fine, she smiles. I hug her reassuringly, muttering something about work stress. I shop for the nursery and Tasha's room, all the while contemplating on calling Aveer.

28

I am completely drained out by the time I reach home. I arrive home to find uncle Baig and Drew sitting on the couch. Shoot, I have totally forgotten that mom has invited them for dinner. This is like the icing on my already disastrous cake. I cannot ignore nor walk away from this situation, so I resign to it.

"Good evening uncle Baig. Hi Drew!"

I sit on the sofa farthest away from Drew, looking for mom and dad. "Aunty and uncle are in the kitchen. And I think Sam has gone to fetch something from his room."

"Ohh, thanks."

"So, you finally here! Did you get the things I asked for?" Mom asked.

"What things?"

Mom gives an exasperated sigh and rolls her eyes, "The list I gave you on the phone? Fruits, dates, condensed milk, etc., the ingredients for the sweets that I have to make for Tasha..."

Holy shit! I slap my forehead and give her a guilty look.

"I am so sorry mom, I forgot! There was too much happening when you called, and half the things did not register."

"Kaira, what's wrong? All good at work?"

"Ya mom, just the meeting with a new publisher was long and exhausting. I am so sorry. I will go in the morning and get everything. Sam is going to get Tasha and Arshi in the afternoon, so you will have time to cook in the morning. And I know Mala aunty is coming to help, so things will work out, huh?"

I smile sheepishly and send her a flying kiss. She shakes her head in angst, like she has given up on me but, naaaa…

"Well, as you have worked that out, what about the tasks you have undertaken? Are you ready? What are you planning to do anyway?"

I point to all the packets near the door.

"I have everything I need in there. As for what I am doing? It's a surprise! Please ensure the maids clean the nursery and Sam's room first thing tomorrow. Also, I need complete privacy, please."

I quickly splash cold water on my face to feel a little fresh before helping mom in the kitchen. Just as I am about to leave, my phone beeps. SMS alert. I gasp as I read the content, 'So, you are not going to forgive me nor talk to me? I really am feeling guilty for my actions. Please accept my apology and reply or call please...'

It must take lots of guts for an arrogant man like him to bend over to impress and pacify someone. Should I reply? I shouldn't… no I should, after all he was sorry and is trying. But what should I type?

'Hi, I am not angry or upset anymore. Yes, it was impulsive, but it's kk.'

I quickly press the 'send' button before I can change my mind. I reach the door and the phone beeps again.

'Thank you. I promise I won't make the same mistake again. Or at least not an impulsive one.' He ends it with a wink emoji.

I scoff at his audacity. He is just too much! I am still smiling when I enter the family lounge, which sure surprises everyone.

"Hey, Kai, that's a sweet smile! What's the reason?" Sam, he just can't help himself, can he?

"Nothing brother dear, just happy."

He slips into a pensive stare. I see his mind working overtime. Luckily dad intervenes, "Kaira, how did the meeting with the devil go?"

"Daaaadd, please! Aveer is just an arrogant self-made man, but no devil. And you were right about hearing everything before reacting. As for the meeting, it went well. He has asked for a no-compete clause with flexible terms and agreed to mine. It was quite a heated meeting, but we were able to agree midway."

Sam quipped jokingly, "Ahhh... Aveer!! So, whatever happened to calling clients by their last names norm, Kaira??"

This raises eyebrows.

I had no idea that my tone, body language, even my expressions had changed. Something which had been missing for a long time was evident to all, even the Baigs. I don't notice dad and Sam exchanging a concerned look, nor mom's reassuring one. But I do see Drew frowning, and just then my phone beeps. Shoot, it's him, again! I feel blood rushing to my cheeks, again.

"Kai, will you help me in the kitchen?"

Thank god for awesome moms! The minute I enter the kitchen I check my message, forgetting that mom is watching too.

'Can we meet for lunch tomorrow? I will get to apologize properly and be sure of your forgiveness.'

I smile at the SMS and look up, straight into mom's questioning eyes. Shit! Busted! She stands with her hands propped on her waist, waiting. I know that look and there is no quipping possible. So...

"It's Aveer, the man I am starting my new business deal with."

"Aveer... the devil, hmm."

"Mooom! Please! Not you too! He is not a devil. He is a nice man, just a tad arrogant. A bit like dad and Sam."

"Hmm..."

I hate this thing about her. She never asks, just patiently waits and watches, knowing I will blurt out everything. I guess all mothers are alike and so is every mother-daughter relationship, huh.

So, barring the kiss and my smitten heart, I tell her everything. Among other things, I mention that he has invited me to lunch tomorrow.

Now that is another thing that really pisses me off about her. She just listens calmly, but never lets on what she is thinking, or how she will react? I nervously wait for her to speak.

"Kai, I think you should invite him tomorrow for dinner. We all will get to meet him. Dad will get a chance to meet the man who brought the spark back in his daughter's life."

"Mom! What on earth are you talking about? I have been fine, in fact, always happy! And as for inviting him, what will I say? Why am I inviting him? We just met three days ago..."

"Kai, sometimes it just takes one look. You reply to his SMS, tell him what you like, but invite him. Trust me."

Of course, I trust mom. Her advice has never gone wrong. I feel butterflies in my stomach. I have never invited a man into my home. Drew was always around, so there was nothing different to it. But with Aveer, everything feels new, different and stronger. I never felt this way with Drew.

I need to think before I reply to Aveer. So, for now, I put the phone aside and sit with everyone for dinner. I listen to dad and uncle's discussion with Sam, ignoring Drew's gaze on me.

Yuck! The look in his eyes is lusty and vicious, making me uncomfortable. What does he want, I wonder? Is he testing waters, trying to get back? OMG! Drew and I are never going to be together, ever.

Drew tries to strike a conversation with me, but Sam manages to avoid it. It is hilarious watching Sam interrupt every time. Even though I am glad, Drew sure is pissed. I think everyone sees Drew's attempts, but chooses to ignore it, letting me handle the situation my way.

I immediately reach for my cell phone once I am in my room. I read his SMS again, and after serious thinking, I write,

'Hi... sorry there were guests at home. Was busy with them. Lunch isn't possible as my niece and sister-in-law are returning from the hospital. Anyway, you don't have to make it up to me with lunch. Its kk,' I send it without expecting a reply. He must be asleep, don't you think?

I go to change into my night clothes. When I pick up my phone about fifteen minutes later, I see two messages from him:

'I know I don't have to make it up to you, but I want to... I want to have lunch with you, spend some time with you. If you are busy tomorrow, we can meet the day after.' Exactly sixty seconds later, the other one reads:

'Or if you and your family would accept my presence, I would love to be part of the occasion. We are, after all, business associates now, aren't we?'

Huh, how should I answer this? Do I want this? Do I want the family to meet him? Who is he to me? Why is he suddenly all around me? So many questions and no answers.

I send him my home address with a 'Looking forward to seeing you tomorrow at 6.30 p.m'. I switch off the phone and lights and doze off into a dreamless slumber...or is it?

29

The next morning, I have difficulty getting up because of another sensual dream. Now, having experienced what a real kiss is like, the dream is more intense, almost panty wetting.

I sigh loudly and dreamily look at the wall clock. I switch on my cell phone. As expected, there is an SMS from him.

'Good morning, Fireball. I hope you slept well. Btw, I accept your gracious invitation. See ya… ttyl!'

Huh, wtf abbreviations?? Just like me!! I am loving this!

'Good morning, Aveer. Yes, I slept well, thank you... did you just use abbreviations?'

'Yaaa, it's a nasty habit. I use them often while speaking and messaging. Why?'

'Nothing… JLT.'

'I think you are lying, but it's kk. Let's discuss when we meet.'

Wow, that sends a zing through my entire being! It's 8.30 a.m., shit! I am late! Again! So much to do before Tasha arrives! I'm omw to the bathroom when the phone beeps. I just could not stop myself from rushing towards my cell phone.

'We are meeting in the evening, aren't we? It's kk if I come, right?'

'Yes. I don't invite anyone I don't want to meet. But now I really need to go, I have a million things to do before my friend and Angel come home. Ciao, ttyl, see you in the evening.' I add a smiley at the end.

I rush through my morning routine. Mom, my saviour, has my coffee ready for me. I quickly gulp my coffee with a toast and ask mom for the list of things she wanted. "That is okay now, Drew took the list from me in the morning."

"Drew? How come he was up so early?"

"I don't know. I could not say no to him, especially when Mala insisted. No harm in giving the boy a chance, what say?"

"Mom, I'm not so sure he has changed. It's just a gut feeling. But I am kk with whatever you say."

I am going towards the nursery when I turn and say, "Mom, I have invited Aveer for the celebrations in the evening. He graciously agreed. So, there is one more person added to the list."

"Hmm... Okay, good. I will let your dad and brother know."

"Mom, please would you also ask them not to pull out their guns. He is just a business associate and nothing more."

"Miss Kaira Kapoor, watch it! It is your dad and brother you are talking about! They know very well how to talk to guests, especially ones interested in their daughter or sister."

I gape at her as she goes about her work. Mr Aveer Mehra is in for a million questions this evening! God help him. I get busy with decorating the nursery and Sam's room. It takes me nearly five hours to get everything as I wanted. Well, perfection is my middle name! I lock the rooms after I am done so that no one would dare to peep in.

When I emerge out of Sam's room, I see Drew. Wtf! Am I going to keep running into him everywhere I turn? So what if he is helping around? I just don't like his presence in my house.

Occasionally like any guest, it's acceptable, but having him like a permanent factor is annoying. I gather my thoughts and say, "Hi, Drew. How's it's going? Need any help?"

"Oh, hi Kai, no I am almost done. Just have these balloons to put up."

"You have done an amazing job here. It looks really nice."

His ears turn red as he says, "Thanks. How about you? You finished with your surprise?"

"Oh yeah, all done! It's actually more than a surprise; it's my gift to the mother and daughter duo."

He gives me a strange look that makes me uncomfortable once again. I quietly go away to find mom. She is in the kitchen. "Mom, I am hungry. What's for lunch?"

"God Kai, stop whining like a baby! There are sandwiches on the counter and freshly squeezed orange juice. Have that for now."

I pout at her and stick out my tongue. I open the fridge and see plenty of bowls covered in foil.

"What have you and aunty made for the evening? Do you need me to make something, a dessert or salad?"

"No Kai, everything is ready. We have mainly stuck to Arabic food, which is Tasha's favourite, and she has been craving it. Mala is getting the desserts and salads. I have also prepared some vegetarian dishes."

"But mom, everyone is non-vegetarian, so why the extra effort?"

"Well we do have a new guest coming, so it's better not to have problems later."

New guest? Ohh she means Aveer!

My mom notices my face brighten as I slip into another 'Aveer fantasy'. Nope! I don't notice her staring at me, nor the slight frown.

I absentmindedly reach out to my cell phone and read his latest messages in the past few hours.

'Hey, what should I get for the baby and mother? And, since it's my first visit, is there a special sweet everyone prefers? Help me! I am clueless!

I burst out laughing reading this last one. I look up to see mom and dad staring at me. Dad, when did he come in?

Shit, what do I do? Why are they looking at me like this? Did I do something wrong?

"What? Why are you both looking at me like this?"

"You just laughed while staring at the phone. We too want to laugh with you..."

My ears are burning as my cheeks turn pink. With dad watching, I get even more nervous. I look at mom in panic with my eyes screaming, HELP! "Husband dear, why don't you check on Sam? See if they have left the hospital, it's nearly 2:30 p.m. Tasha and Arshi need to be settled before the guests start arriving."

Dad shifts his gaze to mom. He knows when he is being dismissed, but he still does as she asks. She looks at me, and instead of answering, I show her Aveer's SMS. A smile lights up her eyes too as she returns my phone.

"Tell him his presence will be good enough. Anyone who can make my daughter laugh like before has given us the most precious gift already."

I blush silently. As I leave the kitchen, I see Drew standing at the door with clenched hands. What happened to him? I am about to ask him when the doorbell rings. It's Tasha and Arshi! I happily rush to the door.

"Welcome! Welcome home!!"

I give Tasha a tight hug and move to take Arshi in my arms. Mom stops me.

"Kai, wait, after this ceremony please. Sam and Tasha, please stand still with Arshi."

She goes in and returns with a beautiful silver plate which has small pots of turmeric, rice, red sindoor and some flower petals. She lights the lamp and circles the plate in front of their faces. With the religious formalities complete, the trio makes a grand entry into their home.

Seeing the balloons and flowers makes Tasha smile, "Kai, this is not you for sure! This has mom written on it totally. You hate balloons!"

"This is actually Drew's handiwork. He has been helping mom decorate the house."

"Thanks, brother. I really love it."

"You are welcome, but I only followed aunty's instructions."

Mom interrupts, "Enough with the thank yous! Kai, let's all see the surprise that you have been working on. That way, Tasha and Arshi can rest before everyone starts arriving."

I fish out the keys to both rooms. When the family enters, the air is filled with happy voices of praise and awe.

The nursery looks like a fairyland, one wall has a picture of a huge palace. Images of angels and windmills adorn the wall near the window. The other wall has all the Disney characters arranged in sequence. Cut-outs of angels are hanging from the ceiling. The ceiling also has glow-in-the-dark stars and moon. Two huge tower clock cupboards stand in a corner. They will hold all Arshi's things.

At the centre of the room, stands a comfortable single couch. The pillows, footstool and comforter complete the picture.

There is a changing table and a crib at one end and a wooden Chester Drawer at the other. Each time the breeze blows through the window, there is a sweet tinkling sound that fills the air. Wind chimes in shapes of stars, moon, angels and butterflies hang at the window.

The loud sound of crying cuts through the happy air. First, I think it's Arshi, but then the hoarse voice made me realize it was Tasha. I rush to her side, "Hey, if you did not like anything, it can be changed! Please, you don't have to sob like this. I am sorry if you did not like it! Tasha…Tasha…"

I look at mom for help, but both she and aunty are laughing. Wtf.

"Shut up Kai, I am not crying because I did not like it. I am crying because I loved it. It is perfect. A dream room for any little girl."

"Wtf...!! You scared the daylight out of me! Have you gone crazy after becoming a mom?"

She is about to start crying again. OMG, what to do?

"Mom! Aunty! Please, help me! She is making me nervous."

"Relax Kai, these are post-delivery symptoms. Hormones, you see! Get used to it."

"Should expect something similar when she sees her room as well? Had I known, I would have waited till this period got over."

Tasha throws a pillow at me and smiles.

"Hey, what's this for?"

"That's for you being #mean #anamazingaunt #awesome friend hashtag…hashtag…hashtag!!! Now let's go to my room! I am dying to see what magic you have done there."

I put my hand around her shoulders and whisper, "Wasn't that way too many hashtags?"

"Shut up!"

I open the door to her room and wait back. This time the shout comes, but not from Tasha. Sam. OMG! I had totally forgotten about him! "What the heck, Kai? Where is *my* room? You have shifted everything! I loved my chair by the window. This is so not fair!"

"Shush Sammy! This is temporary! Right now, your wifey and baby need all the support they can get. We all need to adjust."

I look at Tasha, the look on her face says it all. She loved it!

I have set up everything for her. The bottles, the kettle, bottle warmer and the sterilizer is neatly stacked on the shelf of the new cupboard. Sanitizer is kept handy. A two-way baby monitor is set up for her and Arshi.

Their silence is worrying.

"I either have done a terrible job or such a good one that everyone is speechless...What is it?"

Dad and uncle flank me from both sides and hug me at the same time. They are overwhelmed with happiness.

"Of course, it's the second one sweetheart! You have done an extraordinary job with both the rooms! The attention to detail is so impressive."

Praise from dad always makes me feel an inch taller.

Once everyone leaves the room, I go to Tasha. She is still checking out the nursery. A while later, I feel Tasha wrapping her arms around us, she is filled with gratitude. "Thanks a lot! Everything is so amazing. Even Sam and I could never think of covering all the points. You are simply the best."

I smile and reply smugly, "I know that; but it's always good to hear. Lol. I am glad you loved everything. I couldn't think of a better gift for you both. Why don't you freshen up while I watch over Arshi? Then you both sleep before the guests arrive."

While she moves towards her room, she asks, "Did you finally invite Aveer?"

To Tasha's amazement, I start blushing. Gosh! I am blushing at every given opportunity. What is going on? It's as if I am a giddy-headed teenager again!

I look at Tasha and nod in affirmation. She lets out a loud shout, scaring Arshi.

I pat her to sleep, and exclaim, "Shhh!! Tasha! Look, I had to tell mom almost everything about Aveer. So, she too suggested that I invite him."

She caresses Arshi's little head as the little one goes back to sleep.

"Hmm... That's good... Why do I feel there is something else weighing you down?"

"Yes, you are right."

Should I tell her? I mean, it's just a hunch… maybe I am imagining things.

Tasha sits beside me, "Kai, tell me, even if it's just a passing thought, share it with me."

I take a deep breath and measure my words as I speak, "There is something about Drew… his mannerisms are disturbing me. Something is just not right about him. I am not liking the way he looks at me, nor the way he is trying to get too friendly. Maybe I am overthinking, but I thought it would be better if I mention it to you."

"Don't worry, now that I am home, I will observe him too. You don't have to bother about him. Now let me get ready. You go too, doll yourself up for the special guest." She chuckles and pokes me in the ribs.

"Shut up, Tasha!"

She goes into the bathroom while I sing to Arshi:

"Que será, será
Whatever will be, will be,
The future's not ours to see
Que será, será
Whatever will be, will be…"

30

Once Tasha is ready, I hand over Arshi and go get dressed for the evening. On my way out, I run into Drew. He holds me by my shoulders to stop my fall. I yank myself free and step away from him. Even today, his touch feels repulsive. Is that a flicker of anger in his eyes right now? Why do I even care?

I mumble a thank you and walk away.

I can feel him glaring at me. Is he really upset? But why? I don't realize that Tasha notices and is on alert mode.

I take a quick shower and change into one of my most beautiful dresses. I surprise everyone by wearing something that compliments my frame. It's a brand new dress, the latest design that's in vogue these days. Vibrant shades of red, orange and yellow in a geometric pattern. The colors make my skin look brighter. I accessorise the dress with matching earrings, bracelet and anklet. When I reach the dining room to help lay the table, I am surprised to see Aveer already there. Wtf! I forget everything as I notice his delicious bod in jeans and a yellow colour polo T-shirt. This change comes as a pleasant surprise as I had only ever seen him in suits. He looks so much younger that I can't help but admire him like a lovestruck idiot. Oops!

When he notices me, I see appreciation bring a spark to his eyes. Dear god, I think we look amazing together. How long we stand there staring at each other, I have no idea! We are so engrossed that I don't even notice mom and Tasha in the room. They watch us with awe and admiration. Suddenly the air is filled with Arshi's crying, intervening our staring match, like teenagers.

As soon as I notice mom, I turn my face in embarrassment. I notice Aveer blushing. Aww, he looks cute even while blushing. Wow!

No words have been spoken, yet a flood of feelings has made way to each other's heart. We sure avoid looking at one another now. "Hello, you must be Aveer. I am Kaira's mother, Mrs Nandni Kapoor."

She sticks out her hand, Aveer takes it and kisses her on the back of her hand. He is such a charmer! He has left my mom red in the cheeks too!

"It's a pleasure to meet you, ma'am. I hope I am not intruding..."

"No! Not at all! In fact, I asked Kai to invite you. I have heard a lot about you."

Aveer darts a surprised look at me. I cannot get any redder as I shake my head vigorously. I think he understands that mom knows nothing about the kiss.

"I hope they were good things, because, with your daughter, one can never be sure."

"Hmm... but then you don't know her that well. Yet, whatever she said was in your favour."

He looks at me in disbelief. Mom is impressed with him and likes him. I look at Tasha, but she is staring at Aveer in the same starstruck way as Nikki. Ohh, C'mon! He is not that good looking! What is with these people? OMG, even Zoonie is coming! Will she also behave this way? I slap my forehead in exasperation. Seeing my reaction, Aveer raises his brow. I ignore him.

I am in for an exciting evening for sure. I pinch Tasha and whisper rudely into her ear, "If you are done gawking, let's get going. Guests have started arriving..."

I say this a little loudly so Aveer can hear too. When Tasha still doesn't move, I call out to her husband, "Sam, please take care of your wife. She seems to be lost..."

"Bitch… that was below the belt! It is not my fault that you forgot to mention what a handsome hunk he is? He can enchant anyone with his charming ways. You only have to watch mom to know I am right... huh."

Oops! She is right. Mom never talks like this to anyone, nor does she behave this way, ever. She was stuck by his side, wanting to know as much as she could about him. He has yet to meet dad and Sam and I wonder how they will react. Women are all going gaga over him.

I look down and mutter with indignation,

"Ohhhh my god! I now regret inviting him over."

"If you wish, I can leave now."

Huh? When did mom leave the room? When does Aveer step so close to me? Shoot! What should I do now? I look at Tasha for help, but she is grinning like a moony-eyed idiot while having fun at my expense.

I slowly turn towards Aveer and instead of weighing my words, I blurt out, "You don't need to leave. Just underplay your charm, that's all. The women all around us are falling over themselves because of your sickening charm. I don't want bloodshed on my niece's first day at her home."

"Kaira…!!"

Wtf, didn't mom leave the room? Now I am in a soup! She won't spare me! I look at Aveer with embarrassment and fire in my eyes only to see that he is laughing. It makes me furious; I stomp out of the room before mom can say anything. The laughter that follows my dramatic exit makes me happy. Tasha and mom hitting it off with Aveer is a good sign. Why? Why do I want him to get along with my folks? I am still not ready to delve into these pointed questions.

I go to the drawing room to make sure everything is set. Seeing everything is perfectly laid out I take a step back towards the kitchen only to collide with Mr Aveer…again.

"Are you following me, Aveer? Where is your admiration society?"

"You look so adorable when you are angry and jealous. Well, your mom is checking on the food with another aunty, your sister-in-law has gone to feed the baby, who btw looks like you a lot, very cute and very pink."

Why can't I think of an answer? Why am I blushing constantly? I turn away from him quietly and start to walk away.

"I really like your mom. She is delightful and charming, not at all like you."

I stop in my tracks. "What do you mean? Are you saying I am not sweet and charming, huh? You, mister, are an ass!"

His left eyebrow raises as he looks down at my face. Oops! He is right! My behaviour is surely not charming right now. I scoff and turn towards the kitchen.

"Hey, don't you want to know what I think of you?"

"Nope, not interested!"

I leave him standing there. When I come out of the kitchen about fifteen minutes later, I am shocked.

What? He is friends with the men of the family now? They are talking and laughing as if they are old pals.

I am convinced, Aveer is like Pied Piper. He has everyone in my house eating out of his hand. What is the outcome going to be of this new relationship? What is this relation? Only time will tell.

I look around to check on the others when I feel Drew's piercing eyes staring at me. This creeps me out, but enough is enough! I decide to speak to him directly. I am tired of his new-found obsession. He must know that his antics will not work. "Drew…"

"Yes Kai? How can I help you?"

"Actually, you cannot help me at all. But I can sure help you." I point my finger at him while I shake with anger.

I don't notice Aveer walking towards me. But Drew does notice. A mean smile covers his evil face. It reminds me of… it makes me uneasy, but I stand tall defiantly in front of him. He is still his old self – a wicked wolf, hidden under a sheep's clothing. What is he up to now? I know he was and will remain a bastard.

I answer him with disgust and indignation.

"Stop staring at me. I don't like it. I am ready to forgive and forget for our family's sake, but I will not take this shit from you. I have been ignoring your misbehaviour for a while now. If you don't stop, you be prepared to face the consequences."

He continues smiling as if he was enjoying my discomfort,

"But Kai, I am not doing anything. You are imagining things. Are you sure it is not your way of reconnecting with me? Maybe it is you who still has feelings and are looking of opportunities to reconnecting like old times. After all, you did say you loved me and we did share some good times, right?"

He pauses dramatically and smacks his lips before continuing, "No one better than me knows how vivid your imaginations are. They border on hallucinations. Remember, you had us married a few years back? Now you are playing a new game and blaming me. Don't be coy, be upfront about it. I just might agree this time."

31

His smugness, audacity and viciousness leave me shocked and hurt. I have hoped he had changed, but I am wrong. Damn it! I should have trusted my instincts.

I take a step away from him in revulsion.

His arrogant smile disappears when he sees hatred instead of hurt in my eyes. As I take another step back, I bang into Aveer. Tears of anger and hurt are glimmering in my eyes.

Seeing Aveer standing there shatters me. For the first time in four years, I have let myself feel romance and Drew has destroyed that too. I push Aveer aside and run to my room. The silence in the room doesn't even register. I just want to hide from everyone.

I bury my face in my pillow as I cry. I did not cry when Drew broke my confidence and belief in love. It is the disgust I saw in Aveer's eyes that hurt me deeply.

Till now, I hadn't realized how important Aveer is to me. I cry till my room turns completely dark. I must have fallen asleep while crying. I get up slowly to use the bathroom, feeling as if I have aged by a million years in the past few hours.

It was a stupid move, I should have trusted my instinct and stayed away from Drew. But I just had to confront him, that too on such an auspicious day! I had given that bastard my head on a golden platter so I deserve the humiliation and hurt again. With it, the lesson not to get involved with anyone ever. When I come out of the bathroom, the lights are on, with Tasha and mom awaiting me. Which means that dad and Sam are awake too. Tears gather in my eyes as I look at them beseechingly,

"I am so sorry. I did not mean to spoil everything. I sure did not learn better from past mistakes. I should have just kept quiet and looked the other way. I am sooooo so sorry for humiliating you and dad again."

With this, I burst into tears while crumbling to the floor. I howl so loudly that dad and Sam rush into the room. Dad holds me by my shoulders and picks me up. His warmth and care soothe me a bit. Someone is handing me a glass of water. When I reach out to take it, I notice it is a man. It doesn't seem like dad's or Sam's hand. I look up while sniffling, it's Aveer! Whaaatttt…? Any man in his right mind would have walked away. Is he a fool to stick around? Why is he here?

Fresh tears pour out of my eyes and it pushes dad's patience beyond its limit.

"Enough Kai...! No more crying now. If as much as a tear falls from your eyes, so help me god! We have all endured your dramas occasionally. But today, it wasn't your fault. Maybe the timing was a bit off, but if you felt uncomfortable, I am glad you confronted him head on. That lecherous boy should not have been permitted to cross the threshold of my house. I excused him for Baig, but never again!"

He looks at mom and Tasha as he utters these words. I know he is upset, especially as a scene was created in front of our relatives. I should have curbed my impulse and confronted Drew some other day. It backfired on my family and me.

In between my loud sobs, I exclaim, "I am so sorry, dad. We have kept my stupidity from the world for so long, and today it was all out. All because I could not keep shut for some more time."

"Kaira, you don't need to apologize. Don't bother about the relatives. Your friend here, Aveer, handled the situation very well. In a very dignified manner, he spoke to Drew and made him leave. He cooked up an excuse of your severe migraine to explain your sudden disappearance."

I look at Aveer in surprise. He had saved my family from great humiliation, for which I will remain grateful. I mouth a 'thank you' to which he nods his head and smiles lovingly. We hear Arshi crying; it makes Tasha, Sam and mom leave. Dad pats me on the head and kisses my forehead before leaving the room. Aveer and I are alone now. Aveer has been welcomed into the family, even though I don't know what our relationship is.

The sounds of our breathing are louder than anything else. I can hear voices coming from afar, but the room is in absolute silence. I wait for him to say something, but he just sits by my bed, staring at me. After what seems like ages, I can't take the suspense anymore, so I break the silence.

"Thank you so much for saving my parents from getting humiliated today. I wouldn't have been able to live with myself if that had happened. I don't know what you said or did, but you just gained my deep respect. Thank you."

"Ms Fireball, ever since I met you, I have seen you strong and independent. There has always been a warm halo surrounding your pretty head. I think that's why the name Fireball stuck with me. Seeing you timid, hurt and helpless today made me angry with you."

"Angry at me? I thought you were disgusted with me on hearing what Drew said."

He gapes at me in utter disbelief and irritation, "Why would I be disgusted with you? You were being you, confronting a man you thought was annoying. It takes guts to do that and I am glad you took a stand. But I am angry with you for backing down, for letting him get away with it all. Where was my Fireball when he was taking pot shots at you?"

"Some of those things he said were true. How could I fight that?"

"So what? Even if they were true, they were in the past. To bring them up now was intentional. He was undermining you, and you let him. Why?"

I looked at him meekly, "Because of the humiliation, the hurt, the embarrassment I caused left a huge impact on my self-confidence. I may have made progress in my professional life, but the emotional wounds have still not healed. I thought they had. I thought I was free, but today he took me back to where I was four years ago."

My eyes fall on the wall clock; it is 11 p.m. Shit, it's late! I look at Aveer intending to say good night, but the words get stuck in my throat at the loving look in his eyes. I don't want to name it yet, what if I am wrong, again? But I feel a ray of hope build deep within. I speak, the first thing that comes to mind, "Aveer, it's 11 o'clock. Won't your parents be worrying for you?"

He just starts chuckling, "Sweetheart, I am going to turn thirty in three months. My parents stopped waiting and worrying for me long back. And 11 o'clock is not all that late in a city like Mumbai."

"Hmm..."

After a long pause, it suddenly strikes me what he said, "OMG, you are thirty years old, that is, I mean, pretty old. Why aren't you married till now?"

He looks at me with a queer expression. I am about to question it, when he starts laughing. What begins as a slow laugh becomes boisterous and loud. Hearing this, everyone rushes into the room. He continues laughing even as dad asks him what had happened.

Thinking he is getting hysterical, I start patting him to calm him down. Well, my pat sure works wonders though he continues to chuckle. Thank god, it does not sound hysterical anymore. He keeps looking at me as he finally answers, "I thought you were kidding about her being impulsive and erratic, but NO! You were right! She is that and much more, sir!"

He looks at dad who smiles smugly. I glide my gaze from one to the other, but neither say anything. Aveer gets up and moves to the door. On reaching it, he turns and says, "I will pick you up around noon, and we will have lunch together. Good night for now."

I whisper a good night when I suddenly realize what just conspired. I am being taken to lunch not being asked whether I want to go. What the heck...! I rush out to catch him before he leaves. Dad sees me go, but doesn't stop me, which is strange.

I catch him just before he enters the lift.

"Hey, who says we are meeting for lunch? Sorry, I am busy tomorrow."

"No Fireball, you are not! You are just being difficult because I told and didn't ask you. Well, get used to it."

"Ohh shushhh! You don't get to be my boss. So, if you ever asked nicely, I may just agree, but for now, sorry, no lunch tomorrow!"

I turn away after making my point, only to be hauled right back into his arms. I feel the heat of his breath close to my ears, making me shiver in delight. The touch of his lips between my shoulder and neck causes me to moan softly. When he whispers into my ears, it takes a few seconds to understand what he is saying.

"Don't make such noises or I won't be able to help myself. I promised myself that I will be a thorough gentleman until the time is ours and right. So please don't push me. I am anyway hanging by a thin string."

I don't understand completely what he means by this. However, I do know he is right about emotional and physical control. Here I was, standing outside my house in the arms of a man I have just met. I pull myself away from him and maintain an arm's distance. I look at him, unaware that my eyes are still shining with a passion. I hear him mutter something. I keep looking at him. After a few seconds, he arrives at a decision and shakes his head from side to side.

"Good night Kaira... I will see you tomorrow. Please be ready at noon."

Saying this, he leaves abruptly. Huh? It's like my objection does not matter. Well, he will learn and appreciate the importance of my words from tomorrow. We will see whom he takes to lunch, me or his egoistic invitation.

32

Even though I am wide awake, I am enjoying the coziness and warmth when Tasha joins me in bed. Last night, she had fallen asleep while feeding Arshi, so we have yet to speak about the events. Last night has shaken me up; to top it, Aveer has me tied in knots.

"Good morning, Ms Celebrity! Move over, I want to join in. I haven't slept a wink. Arshi was crying all night.."

"Hmm, btw, why are you calling me Ms Celebrity?"

She settles herself in my bed before she updates me on the events after I left. Each word pleasantly shocks me, but brings an inner glow with it.

"When you went to confront Drew in your usual war mode, I had just come out of the room. Seeing your expressions worried me, so I was coming to you, but saw Aveer break away from the group to follow you. I had not expected Drew to be up to his old tricks, so his words left me stunned too. I was about to intervene when Aveer signalled me to stop. I wondered why…?"

She looks at me for an answer.

"He said that he was waiting for me to hit back at Drew. He did not expect me to cower or back down," I tell her.

"Hmm, anyway, I couldn't take it anymore and was about to take Drew's case when you turned. Seeing horror and humiliation written all over your face scared me. And, it brought such fury to Aveer's face that I think even Drew got scared."

"Fury? I thought I saw pure disgust towards me."

"Are you mad? Your man was going to follow you to your room. But knowing that it could spoil the festive atmosphere and raise questions, he turned to Drew. He quietly escorted Drew out of the lounge straight to the door, and warned him about coming anywhere in your vicinity. Dad and Sam witnessed everything and didn't say a word when they saw the possessive anger on Aveer's face. They silently went inside to tend to the guests."

The minute Tasha had said Aveer was angry and not disgusted, I had jumped up and sat on the bed. The man I barely know was fighting for me... Wow! The man I had just met three days ago was helping keep my family and my reputation intact. Whereas the man who was part of my extended family didn't care nor have any respect for his family, let alone mine. "You know Kai, last night Aveer gained everyone's respect and approval. He was not only liked by dad and Sam, but even my father was impressed by him. As for our mothers, they are women, and he sure can blind us all with his sexy smile and elegant manners. We all really liked him, Kai."

I look at Tasha and seek encouragement to pursue the unknown. And if I am honest to myself, I too want to. But I don't say anything. I get up to get ready.

As I collect my stuff, Tasha asks, "Hey what you are doing?"

"Ma'am, I am getting ready for work. You have the luxury to sleep, but I have to work."

"But I thought you were going out for lunch with Aveer."

"I would have if he had asked, but he ordered. You know, I don't follow orders."

Saying this, I go for my shower. I don't realize that my friend would sneak behind my back and tell Averr thirty minutes later, I am all ready and set to go. As I leave the room, I get back to pick up my cell phone. I check if he has sent a message, but alas! Nothing! I shrug off my disappointment and march out nevertheless. If he doesn't wish to speak, then nor do I. I enter the dining room only to come to an abrupt halt. Right there on the table, Aveer sits with the rest of my family, enjoying breakfast! Even Arshi is there, sleeping sweetly in mom's arms. Wtf!

"Good morning Kaira, you look lovely this morning!"

I gape in wonder. But to my utmost amazement, dad continues reading his newspaper, mom just smiles and Sam, who usually would pass a comment, continues eating, huh!

Have I walked into the wrong family?

I look at Aveer; his eyes are dancing with pure mischief. I must look like an idiot with my mouth slightly open, gaping at everyone. Tasha comes out of the kitchen with a cup of coffee for me.

"Oh, you're here, here take your coffee! I need to settle Arshi. Hey, Aveer, you need anything else?"

I hear his muffled 'no' as if he is controlling his laughter. Now I am getting pissed. What the heck is going on here? I look at him fiercely and ask through my clenched teeth, "What on sweet mother earth are you doing here? It is only 9 a.m., nowhere near lunch time..."

He steps closer and whispers, "I love it when you go all Brit when you are angry. Seeing this fire first thing in the morning has just made my day. As for what I am doing here, well, I was invited."

"Invited? Who invited you?"

"Me..."

The answer comes from the last person I expected. Sam.

"Wtf..."

"Kai! Watch it! We have a baby in the room and the parents."

"Oh, shut up Sammy! Arshi is long gone and mom and dad are now used to us squabbling. Why would you invite him to breakfast? I mean, you just met him and don't know him from Adam, so?"

From the corner of my eye, I see the rascal enjoying our tiff and smirking.

"Well, sometimes it takes only one meeting to know someone and to like him. Being a stranger, he not only helped us from embarrassment, but even stayed till the end, for you. So, thanking him is what people who live in civil society would do. Oh wait, did I say civil society?"

Oh shoot! I don't need this. I pick my tote bag and move to the door, ready to leave. Sam calls out, "Hey, where are you going? We have a guest."

"No Sammy, *you* have a guest! I am leaving for work. Bye!"

I leave a stunned Sam behind me. I hear a loud laugh after my exit. I know it is Aveer. He seems to find humour in everything I say or do. Well, hahaha to him too. The lift stops on the sixth floor. Drew enters with a suitcase. I turn my head and ignore him. I can feel his gaze, but I refuse to give him the satisfaction that he was being noticed. His brash behaviour was still fresh. I wait impatiently waiting for the lift to stop. The minute it does, I rush out towards my bike.

I am just about to start my bike when I hear Drew. I do not realize he had followed me. He comes and stands in front of my bike and starts speaking, "I know you don't wish to speak to me. Please, just two minutes of your time, that's all I am asking."

I look at him angrily. Is that regret that I see in his eyes? Is it even genuine? He takes a deep breath and says, "Thanks. I know I don't deserve it, but still, I appreciate it... I truly am sorry, and this time I am not mouthing the words, but I really mean them. I was an arrogant jerk, thinking I could manipulate you into loving me."

I look at him with surprise as he continues to speak, "Kai, you and I both know, what you felt for me was not love, it was teenage infatuation. I should have nipped it in the bud itself. However, I was too pompous and full of myself. Seeing the look in your eyes for Aveer hurt my ego. I was living in a bubble that made me believe you could only be in love with me. I was jealous when I realized you had never ever looked at me like that. That's what made me react the way I did."

Huh! Did he just say that he saw love in my eyes for Aveer? Anyway, the sincerity in his voice compels me to forgive him.

I must forgive and forget, for my own sake. If I don't, I will never be able to close this chapter and start a new one. I look at Drew wondering what I ever loved about him. "You are right. I need to forgive you first, so that I can forgive myself. If I don't, then the guilt will continue to suffocate me. So yes Drew, I forgive you, for everything. And I also wish you the very best in life."

"Thanks, Kaira. I am glad I got this chance to speak to you before I returned to Dubai. Leaving the country is the best thing I can do to ensure everyone I love manages to live in peace. Even mom is very hurt and not speaking to me. Well, all the best to you too. Have a lovely future."

We hug each other lightly.

"ATB, Drew. Bye."

I ride off, feeling lighter than before.

33

I don't look back, so I don't know what happens after I leave.

My ATB confuses Drew. He mutters to himself, "ATB… what the heck does that mean?"

"All the best." Drew looks back to see Aveer standing there.

"Since how long have you been eavesdropping?"

"I have been here since you came out of the lift. Just did not want to interrupt."

"Ahhh... you are the protective watchdog, aren't you?"

Drew watches Aveer clench his fists, but he maintains a miraculous calm while he replies, "Ohh, no worry about that! I know she wouldn't give you the time if she didn't want to. I trust her. She is too straightforward to play games. In fact, it is you who reminds me of a snake, ready to strike at the first opportunity."

"Then why eavesdrop?"

"My Fireball is capable of fighting her demons. And her dignified bravery just now proves me right and just makes me love her even more."

They exchange angry looks. Drew's grunts of regret and jealousy is apparent.

Aveer steps away and starts to walk off towards his car. Suddenly he starts thinking aloud, forgetting about Drew and where he is.

"In Kai, I know I have found the perfect partner. With her, my search has ended. I didn't realise I was searching, until her. She is the light and joy of my life. I have never enjoyed laughing, acting crazy or arguing with anyone in the last thrity years of my life. But in three days, I have seen so many different shades of my personality. I love it, even though it surprises me."

He turns around only to watch Drew walking away with his shoulders drooped, his train of thoughts continues, "I feel sorry for Drew. He burnt his boats while trying to make my life miserable. I hated the way he was eyeing Kaira yesterday. Bastard! His selfish actions worked in my favour. I guess I can forgive him a bit. Kaira's family loves and respects me now. They even invited me for breakfast today. Tasha and Sam seem to love me too. Especially Tasha, who sure can help build a case before Kaira. Kaira's friend means the world to her. Hmm. How do I convince Fireball now, that we are meant to be together."

He opens his car door, still lost in thoughts, "Last night, when she enquired about my marital status, I laughed it off. The question did worry me though. Had I missed the bus? I had a long discussion with my grandfather who is more of a friend to me.

He heard me out and just said,

"Aveer, life is beckoning you, grasp it with both hands while you still have time. Remember, we never get second chances. Your parents' ways towards married life should not affect your ideas about holy matrimony. Start having thoughts and dreams of your own."

A hand on my shoulder stops me just as I am about to sit in my car.

It was Drew, who told me, "I know I am a bastard, but I genuinely think you and Kai make a great pair. I could never have been able to handle the energy within her. I wish you both the very best for your future."

"That almost sounds like a goodbye."

He chuckles faintly, "Chillax!! It's only temporary till everything settles down. Of course, I will be back. I may be the black sheep, but I am still family."

"Hmm... Well, TC... ATB."

Shaking his head Drew exclaims, "You both really have a lot in common, sure meant to be kinds."

As Drew turns to leave to his waiting taxi, Aveer wonders whether he is helping him or scaring him away.

Either way, Aveer now has a plan… will it be the perfect one? Only time will tell.

34

I reach ECL, relaxed and calm. Forgiving Drew seems to have finally liberated my soul. I feel as if I am reborn. My heart yearns for a blissful future with a man who respects me and loves me unconditionally for my craziness. I want to love a man with whom I can appreciate and argue without an ego clash. Have I encountered him already?

"Aveer…"

"Huh, Nikki, what's with you? Why are you taking the devil's name in vain?"

"Kai, I said hi to Aveer."

Shoot, Aveer is standing right behind me! What is he doing here? I turn so fast that I trip and finally I meet mother earth! Everyone laughs at my plight. My eyes are on Aveer. I gasp as I see him holding a 5-foot-tall teddy bear. Wtf…? What now?

"Hi, I would have saved you as always, but as you can see, my hands are full. Btw, how can a person standing straight up just crumble to the ground like this?"

I grunt and scoff while dusting myself.

"Ohh, shut up Aveer! What are you doing here? You are supposed to be at my home having breakfast with my family."

"Well, I am here with this peace offering."

His tone makes me embarrassed! Hurrump! How does he manage to do this every time? Why do I find his antics charming? He is so annoying, isn't he? I walk away before I make a bigger fool of myself. The balcony on the top floor is my favourite space.

I don't notice Aveer standing by the door watching me. God knows for how long he has been standing there. I open my eyes when I feel as though I am being watched. I mutter to myself, "Hmmn Kaira, it's a dream, your Mystery Man is back." I look at him moony-eyed. Aveer gasps slightly and smiles. What is in his eyes? Is it passion or lust. Wait, is it…love…no! It can't be. His intense look makes my heart palpitate. "What is going on here? I have never felt this way ever! I am losing control over my thoughts and emotions... we just met. How is it even possible?"

Shoot, I was rambling loudly! Aveer rushes to my side. He holds my hand tightly, "There is no time span for falling in love. And this, sweetheart, is love! I am old enough to be sure that it is. Fear is natural, I am feeling it too, but together we can overcome every storm, Kaira."

I gasp, "OMG, you said 'the word' so easily! I can't even use it in my thoughts. How can you be so sure it is…I mean… huh...?"

He looks deep into my eyes and says, "I just know. You, Kaira, are the woman I love. You made me realize there is a world beyond work. For you, I could take unlimited detours, just to see you. You are the woman who can outsmart me in the middle of the road, making me forget everything. And yes, you bring laughter and colours into my life. You, Kaira, are '*the woman*' for me…my woman."

OMG…he is on his knees! Aveer Mehra is bravely declaring love! I am humbled beyond expression. Is he ready to bond with an erratic, impulsive, crazy woman like me? Like an idiot, instead of replying, I ask, "What about your parents, your family? What is their view?"

He squeezes my hand, takes a deep breath and says, "Kaira, my family is not like yours. My parents have no time for me. They are too busy in their social life to be bothered about who I bring home as my wife. I have a grandfather who means the world to me. He said that he would love to have you in the family. So, Ms Fireball, I don't want to let go. Will you jump in with me?"

Say *yes* Kaira!! Say yes!

My mind screams out loudly!

"I need to speak to my family, especially Tasha. She will kill me if I say yes before telling her."

He lets go of my hand and takes a step back apologetically.

"Please, Aveer, don't feel bad... I am not saying no; I am just saying I need my family around when I..."

I trail off as he looks up with hope. When I don't complete my statement, he makes a grouchy face and turns away.

I stand up, move closer and softly kiss him on his cheek, "How's that for a sorry?"

He smiles and offers his other cheek as well.

"Lol, don't get too smart! One is enough for now!"

I wink at him and proceed towards the library. He stops me from opening the door.

"I won't let you get away that easily sweetheart."

He bends down and kisses me passionately on my lips. After a while, I playfully push him away, but he moves closer and whispers in my ears, "See you at your home in the evening, I will get my Grandad along too. You can give me your answer in front of them."

He gives me another kiss and leaves. Huh, what just happened? Have we just confessed to being in love? I pull myself together and enter the library. What???

The teddy bear is sitting in the centre with a massive card in its lap. It is open for the whole world to read:

'I, Aveer Mehra, am deeply in love with Ms Kaira Kapoor. I would be honoured if she agrees to enter my life and stay there for eternity.'

35

I read the message again and again. Each time, my smile grows till it turns into a happy grin while my eyes shine with pure joy.

I grab the card and rush home. Do I hear the whistles and catcalls? No, I don't! I fly home.

I quickly park and run to the lift. What if dad says no? I take a deep breath, open the door, only to be surprised at seeing Sam there.

"Hey Sammy, why aren't you and dad in office?"

"We are expecting important guests in the evening. So, we had to stay back for the preparations."

"Guests? Today? In the evening? Who? What? Why?"

"Huh? Kaira? What is wrong with you? Why are you talking like this? We are home for a reason, but what about you? You never leave the Café before 9 p.m.?"

"I had something important to discuss… with mom... Where is she?"

"She is in the kitchen."

Huh? What's this? It looks like they are preparing meals for a king. Even dad is busy helping.

"Mom, who is coming in the evening. I mean, when are the guests coming?"

"Kai, I don't have time for chitchat. If you can help, good; if not, then please let me finish."

That was rude! Who could be so important? Mom never ignores me! I move towards Tasha's room when mom calls, "Listen, Kai, if you are going to be home, then please dress well. Maybe a nice Indian outfit for a change."

Huh, Indian dress, that means some of dad's old friends are coming. Hmm, shit, I will need to call Aveer and cancel for the evening. He can't be here while there are guests at home. It will be embarrassing.

"Mom, what time are your guests arriving?"

"They should be here by 5 p.m. That means you have about two hours to get ready and lay the table."

"I am going to meet Tasha first!"

"Miss Kaira Kapoor! Come back here. Don't you dare disturb Natasha! She has just fed Arshi and is taking a nap. It is going to be a long evening, so she needs the rest."

Great, I don't even get to talk to my bestie for help. Now what? Well, first things first, let me call Aveer. I call him, but he does not answer. I SMS him after the fourth call goes unanswered, 'I am so sorry. We have to cancel the plan. Guests are expected, with them around we can't talk."

Ten minutes later, my phone beeps with his message.

'Kk.'

Shoot! I hurt him! Did I? Does 'kk' mean that he is okay with it and understands, or he is upset or … is it worse? I pace across the room trying to calm myself. But when nothing works, I go out to help mom to stop myself from thinking of Aveer.

Half an hour before the guests are due, mom sends me to get ready. What is so special about today? Why Indian? Why now? Well, I always follow mom's orders, so…

I pick out a purple, ethnic salwar suit with the dupatta in a myriad shade of purple and blue, complete with golden stripes. I team the dress with a traditional bindi that seals the look.

When mom sees me, tears well up in her eyes, "Why are you so emotional, mom? I have worn this suit before, haven't I? For Mr Jethwani's daughter's wedding last year, remember?"

She replies between her sniffles, "It's just that you are looking very magnificent today."

Ooookkkay!! Something is not right!

"Where is Tasha? Is she up?"

"Natasha is getting ready. Sam is with Arshi. Why don't you take care of her and send Sam back? I need to speak to him."

I go to the nursery where Sam is sitting on the chair holding a sleeping Arshi.

"Hey, give her to me. Mom is calling you…go!"

Sam gently places the baby in my arms and leaves quietly. Huh? Why is everyone so cagey today? Have I done something wrong? I pensively sit on the chair and cradle my lovely niece. Holding Arshi brings me peace. I love the feel of her tiny soft body cuddling to me. Her face is so innocent, she sleeps without worldly worries. I am lost in her sweet world.

Huh! I suddenly get a prickly feeling of being watched. I look up to meet my favourite chocolate brown eyes. Time stands still till Tasha clears her throat and punctures the mood.

Aveer bends and whispers a soft 'hi' into my ears. The heat of his breath warms my ear, causing it to tingle.

I whisper back, "Aveer… you… here?"

"You invited me. So, here I am!"

"But, you sent a rude 'kk', so… how…?"

I hear giggles in the doorway. Everyone is watching us. I start blushing.

"He is the guest, huh?"

"No, actually it's my Grandpa! He is the guest of honour."

OMG! It is really happening. Aveer is here with his grandfather. Are they really going to talk about our wedding?

Nervous shivers run through my body. Tasha lunges forward and takes Arshi from me. Mom puts her arms around me. Meeting Aveer's Grandad is an amazing experience. He is full joie de vivre with a knack of making everyone comfortable and happy. The minute I meet him, he gives a tight hug and whispers 'welcome to the family'. The whole family chit chats animatedly. Baig uncle and Mala aunty are also there.

Aveer and I steal a moment and go to my room. The minute he closes the door, I start complaining, "That was mean! In fact, everyone was mean. All of you hid this from me. Everyone ignored me this afternoon. You didn't answer my calls and replied curtly. Do you know how many doubts ran through my mind in that one moment? It was unbearable."

As I continue with my whining, he pulls me in his arms and covers my mouth with his. I open my eyes so wide. I am completely taken aback! After a few seconds I realize that I am kissing him back. Our lips unite and move in unison as if slow dancing to soulful music. His tongue touches mine and I explode. I arch my back and thrust my bosom closer to him. When he nips the side of my lip, I cannot stop the moan. His lips leave mine to gently kiss me all over my neck and chest. I go weak in the knees, but his strong grip keeps me steady. He keeps returning to my lips for more and more. With every nip and every suck, I feel myself merging with his soul while drowning in emotions.

We are lost in time when a knock and push on the door rudely wake us out of our fantasy land. Aveer, who has been pressed against the door moves back, while I jump to the other side of the room. What if it is dad or Sam, shoot! Luckily, it's just Tasha. She looks at us both and then straddles to the dresser, pulls out a tissue and hands it over to Aveer.

"That lipstick colour suits Kai better than you. You lovebirds better straighten up and come out before anyone notices." She winks and walks out, chuckling gleefully.

I have never seen a grown man blush as fast as Aveer does. It totally turns me on!

Of course, I am embarrassed by Tasha's remarks, but this soft, mushy feeling is far lovelier. I see a new side to Aveer, this time a vulnerable one. He steps closer and whispers, "Ms Fireball, shall we leave? Hmm? Unless you have something else in mind." He runs his fingers across my back.

I look at him in false indignation, despite the shiver that runs down my back. I am about to reprimand him when he distracts me again, "Could you check if the lip colour has been wiped off? Your dad or my Granda shouldn't notice it. That would be very embarrassing for both of us... wouldn't it?"

I blush and notice a light cut on his lower lip. Oops!

"Umm... sorry, there is a slight cut on your lower lip... and just wipe off the left side of your lip."

He smiles and hands me his tissue. I carefully wipe off the remaining lip colour, all the while feeling his warm breath on my face. When I hand over the tissue, he gently kisses the back of my hand and then guides me to the lounge.

Aveer and his Granda stay beyond dinner. Everyone is having fun, so the passage of time didn't matter. Granda may be about 80, but he didn't look a day beyond 60. He is active and fit. Like a wise owl, he looks over his family night and day. When they are ready to go, he pats me on my head.

"I am glad you entered my grandson's life. You are just right for him. God bless you!"

I hug him tightly, "It is an absolute honour to meet you, sir."

"It's Granda for you, sweetheart. Sir is too formal for a family member. Don't you think?"

I nod silently, while blushing. Everyone walks out, Aveer stays back, "You free for brunch tomorrow, at your café?"

"Sure. I will be there only."

"Actually, don't go to the café tomorrow. Let me pick you at noon, and we'll go together. Will that be okay? Please?"

"Well, since you ask so nicely… okay!"

"You saucy minx!"

He kisses me lightly on my forehead and leaves.

36

The next morning, I wake up from a deep slumber to the harsh ringing of the phone. It's my alarm. I switch it off, but the noise persists.

Uff! Wtf…?

Oops! It's a call from Aveer!

"Yes Aveer, what do you want?"

"Good morning Fireball. If you ask me in that sexy voice, all I want is, *you!*"

Wtf... it's not even morning, it's dark outside the window.

I don't realize that I have spoken aloud until the voice at the other end answers, "It's 5.15 a.m. Why? You not up yet?"

I blare loudly into the phone, "Are you out of your bloody mind? Who gets up at this hour? You enjoy romancing the sunrise. I am sleeping."

I hang up. It rings again!

"Urrghh!!! Aveer!!! What now?"

"What time do you get up? I mean, I should know, right?"

"8 a.m. or after. Nite nite!"

Shoot! My sleep has vanished! I might as well get dressed. I take a refreshingly long shower and change into my tracks. Everyone stops in their tracks as they notice me entering the family room.

"Good morning family. Mom! Coffee please!"

"Miracle! An absolute miracle! Oh, My Gooooddd!!! Miss Kaira Kapoor graces us with her esteemed presence at 6:30 a.m. Impossible has been made possible!!"

"Cut the dramatics, Sam. It doesn't suit you!!"

"C'mon Kai. Even Arshi decided to arrive during the day; she knew any time before 8 a.m., and her aunt wouldn't have been present to greet her."

I laugh sarcastically, "This is why I don't get up early! Your crazy jokes kill my morning fun."

As I move towards the kitchen, I see dad's shoulder shaking vigorously, huh? Is he laughing behind the paper? I stomp my feet like a two-year-old.

"Et tu Dad?"

Even mom is trying hard to stop herself from laughing as she asks, "Kai how did this miracle happen?"

"Mom! It's no miracle, it's a one-time event. Aveer woke me up at the alien hour of 5:15 a.m."

Oops! I feel heat enter my cheeks. I look down in sheer embarrassment. I never will learn to think before I talk, will I?

I am clearing the table when my phone beeps. Why isn't he calling? Why the SMS? 'Good morning Sunshine! Hope you are up and fresh now. A slight change in plans. Work calls. Let's meet for early dinner. Will pick you at 7:30 p.m. XOXO'

I have been stood up! Hmm, its kk. I might as well go to the café, but mom stops me from going on some random pretext. In the evening, mom gets ready for a last-minute social obligation with dad. Sam was going to be late at work. Mala aunty was coming to keep Tasha company. When I enter my room, I am surprised to see a new dress spread on the bed.

It is the most exquisite dress I have ever seen! Turquoise blue, off-shoulder, with three strings of freshwater pearls around the neck like a choker. The tiny sequins scattered all over the dress make it sparkle. It was perfect!

"Whose dress is that mom?"

"Mine! Kai, love has made you lose all sense! It is for you, silly girl!"

"But why? It's beautiful, but too formal for a modest dinner. Btw, when did you buy it?"

"Shhh! It's perfect for the occasion! But sadly, I did not buy it. Aveer did. I only helped with your size."

"Occasion? What occasion Mom? I am just going for dinner."

"Kai! It's your first official date. You have never ever been on one. I feel like an American parent, sending her child on a prom date! Get dressed and go have a wonderful time."

Aww…Aveer is a sweetheart and my mom, she is a total darling, and this dress… it shouts romance and love.

Hmm…well then, I too should make an effort. I go the extra mile and create magic with make-up; enhancing my eyes with a hint of colour and mascara. For a moment I feel like those Instagram models who promote make-up. The final look is awesome! For the first time in years, I feel beautiful from within. I strap on my pumps, the only ones I own, matte silver and gold mix colour that goes with all my dresses.

When I step out of the room, I see bewildered looks on every face.

"Kai, you look like Cinderella!"

Huh! Is that really Sammy?

I see dad avert his gaze to hide his tears.

Mom is beaming with joy and pride seeing her daughter all dolled up. I again get a feeling that something is going on that I am not aware of.

But for now, I am soaking in the glory when Tasha shouts!

"*Oh my god!* You look stunning. I knew you had it in you, but this is amazing! You actually look like a grown woman."

The room is filled with mirth! I give her an irritated look and open my mouth to curse her. The doorbell saves her from my wrath.

"Hey, Aveer... come on in!"

Aveer stops in his tracks, causing Sam to bang into him.

He looks at me, awestruck.

Dad clears his throat and we come back to reality.

I flash a thousand-watts smile, not only because I look beautiful, but because I feel beautiful. Never felt this way before, it is amazing.

He holds out his hand and softly asks, "Shall we?"

The fact that he asks and does not state the request make me all mushy. I feel in total sync with my partner. It seems like a lifetime has passed instead of just four days. I almost feel like I know him without knowing him. I place my hand in his with full trust and confidence for my first date.

We drive to a place twenty minutes from home. Aveer has reserved a table for two at The Louvre, one of the most sophisticated fine dining restaurants in Mumbai. We are seated in the private coupe where the service is personalized and is perfect. But what is missing is, words.

We haven't spoken since we left home. I have felt his gaze on me while he drove, but no words are exchanged. I am nervous and he echoes my thoughts, "I have never seen you this quiet. It's refreshing."

I roll my eyes at him and smile.

"Don't get too used to it, mister! It is a very rare occurrence. I have never ventured into such a classy restaurant, nor have I dressed so formally. Even for Sam and Tasha's wedding, I was underdressed, but that's how I like it.

"Hmm, so many firsts! Are there more?"

"Hmm, this is my first date, and then there is the ki..." I trail off and quickly eat my words.

"What ki...?

Should I say it?

I break eye contact and look around. When I look back at Aveer, his eyes have not left me.

"Why is the restaurant empty? I know it recently reopened, but why is it so dead?"

"Umm, maybe because I booked the whole place for us??"

"Why? I mean, it's sweet, but won't it be a loss for the owners?"

Oops! Childish question, especially from a businesswoman like me.

He seemed to love my child-like behaviour, "Relax sweetheart! It is no loss to the owners. One night wouldn't matter."

"What do you mean?"

"Well, my family owns this and a few more restaurants like this one..."

Wtf...? How rich is this man, really? "Listen, I know it's a surprise, and we have not spoken about these small things, but that's what our relationship is all about – discovering each other."

"Wow, you really are rich! The Prada type rich, holy moly!!"

"Prada type?"

I narrate how Nikki spoke about him after their first meeting. He laughs heartily, and just then the waiter brings champagne for us. We toast to our future. As I take the sip and sigh, he says those three words. I am thinking when will I get myself to say them, when the phone rings.

I answer it only because it's from the café. I check the time, it's 9 p.m.; the café should be closed by now. I wonder who is calling. I hear a panicked Pete. He is blabbering. I can not understand a single word of what he is trying to say.

"Pete, Pete, please calm down. I can't understand. Take a deep breath and begin again."

I hear him take a few breaths before he talks again, "Kai, I need you at the café right now! Please! I can't solve this issue alone. Robin and Nikita have left for the day, and their phones are switched off."

"Can't it wait till tomorrow?"

"Would I trouble you if it could? Come fast, please…!"

The fact that Pete and Robin share an apartment doesn't register my panicked mind.

As soon I hang up with Pete, I exclaim, "I am sorry Aveer, I need to be at the cafe. Something has gone wrong, and Pete is panicking. Can we leave immediately?"

Aveer gets up immediately and we rush to ECL. We reach to a totally dark place. An eerie silence surrounds the property. Wtf! I clasp Aveer's hand so tightly, I guess I leave nail marks on his soft skin.

I mutter nonstop, "Why is it sooo dark? Where is Pete? Oh god, oh god, please please let everything be okay..."

I leave Aveer's hand and run into the café, praying all the time. My heart is filled with worry and it's pounding fast. I yank open the door shouting. "Pete, Pete where are you? What's this fragrance? Shit, what has happened here? Pete, switch on the light… where are you, bro? Are you fine?"

I circle across the café, trying to find my way in the dark. It doesn't strike me to use the torch on my cell phone.

Suddenly the lights go on, blinding me for a split second. A shower of flowers descends on me. "Surprise!!"

My friends, family, including Aveer's Granda were standing there, looking at me excitedly. The whole place is decorated with festoons, decorative lights and flowers. There are roses, lilies and orchids everywhere I look. The whole place feels like paradise.

I look at Aveer in question, but he is nowhere to be seen. I see him standing at the stairs, the place we first met. OMG! He has the mike in his hand!

"Before I address this lovely lady who stands before me in wonder, I want to thank you all for making this possible. Thank you, Nikita, Zoonie, Robin and Pete – you guys are ever so dependable! Thank you everyone, from the bottom of my heart."

Saying this, he goes to mom and dad for blessings. Mom places her hand on his head and kisses him on the forehead. Dad hugs him and pats him on the shoulder. My friends, colleagues and close relatives, everyone who mattered were here.

Wtf…even Tasha is here with Arshi!! She is supposed to be under house arrest for forty days as per Indian tradition for a new mom? Ohh wow!

My heart beats like crazy as Aveer strides towards me.

"Miss Kaira Kapoor, it has been five days, twelve hours, forty-five minutes and about fifteen seconds since you crashed into me. But I feel I know you since eternity. I have never experienced so many emotions in my life as I did in this period. I would love to live my life on the edge, swirling around this whirlpool of emotions till my last breath."

He stops in front of me. I hold my breath in anticipation. He takes my hand and leads me where my family is standing. Surrounded by the family, all the while looking at me, he finally asks.

"With all their blessings, I would be honoured if you, Ms Kaira Kapoor accept this token of my love and remain with me till eternity."

He fishes out the most perfect ring ever – a 3 carat teardrop solitaire!

Good looking, caring, ambitious, respectful and romantic - is this guy for real? To top it, he is rich and a family man too! Wow! When did I get sooo lucky?

As he awaits my answer, I take the ring I see in mom's hand and surprise him by kneeling. "Mr Aveer Mehra, you too have shown me a lot in this short span of time. Even things I had stopped believing in – you made them happen. Above everything, you have shown me how to express with panache."

He bends slightly to pick me up, but I shake my head lightly and continue, "So, Mr Aveer Mehra, would you do me the honours of always being as you are? Always love me, surprise me and charm me this way. With this ring, will you accept my love and commitment to you for eternity?"

Aveer bends down as the crowd goes, 'Aww…' in unison. The atmosphere is filled with claps, whistles and joy. He picks me up and scoops me in his arms. "You, my dear Fireball, are going to be the death of me, but I still love you…"

"I love you too, Aveer…"

Yes, I finally say it, and the time couldn't have been more perfect.

Epilogue

It is a well-known fact that nothing in life ends till there is hope. One should keep hoping till the last breath. Till we breathe, we have a chance to believe, to dream and to make new realities. Always pave your path forward, and ways will open for you. I may have stopped looking for love, but I learned to look ahead and make new ways. I learned, fight is always better than flight. In return, god blessed me by opening the doors of love in my path forward.